Pirate's Island

JOHN ROWE TOWNSEND

Pirate's Island

ILLUSTRATED BY DOUGLAS HALL

London
OXFORD UNIVERSITY PRESS
1972

Oxford University Press, Ely House, London W. I

GLASGOW NEW YORK TORONTO MELBOURNE WELLINGTON
CAPE TOWN IBADAN NAIROBI DAR ES SALAAM LUSAKA ADDIS ABABA
DELHI BOMBAY CALCUTTA MADRAS KARACHI LAHORE DACCA
KUALA LUMPUR SINGAPORE HONG KONG TOKYO

© John Rowe Townsend 1968
First published 1968
First published in this edition 1972

ISBN 0 19 272034

Printed in Holland
Zuid-Nederlandsche Drukkerij NV
's-Hertogenbosch

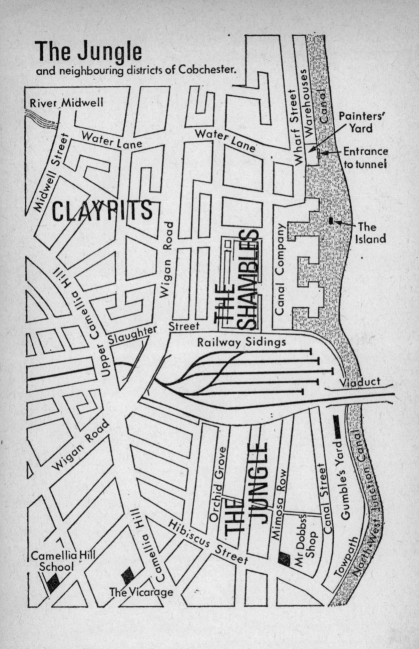

The Jungle

and neighbouring districts of Cobchester.

River Midwell

Water Lane

Water Lane

Midwell Street

Wharf Street

Warehouses

Canal

Painters' Yard

Entrance to tunnel

CLAYPITS

Wigan Road

THE SHAMBLES

Canal Company

The Island

Upper Camellia Hill

Slaughter Street

Railway Sidings

Viaduct

Wigan Road

Orchid Grove

THE JUNGLE

Mimosa Row

Canal Street

Gumble's Yard

North-West Junction Canal

Camellia Hill

Hibiscus Street

Mr Dobbs's Shop

Towpath

Camellia Hill School

The Vicarage

Chapter 1

'You know what he puts in his sausages? Scrapings off the floor!'

'Sawdust and dead dogs!'

'Stinking fish!'

In the back alley behind Camellia Hill council school, in the spring of 1946, a gang of boys gathered round Gordon Dobbs, the pork-butcher's son, taunting him.

'He doesn't, he doesn't!' protested Gordon, half-way to tears.

''Course he does,' said Tim Ridgeway, a small scrawny boy with a surprisingly low, rough voice. ''Course he does. Swill, that's what your dad makes his sausages from. And swill, that's what they're fit for.'

'It's not true, Tim Ridgeway!'

'Everyone says your dad made his pile in the war, when things were scarce,' said Alan Manning. Alan was a big, red-haired boy of fourteen, the oldest of the group. 'And now he owns his shop and a posh van and a row of houses. That's what they say, Porky.'

Tim Ridgeway pushed to the front.

'It's true, isn't it, Porky?' he demanded. 'While everyone else was in the Army, your dad stayed at home, selling muck and getting rich.'

'He was turned down for the war,' said Gordon with dignity. 'He was Grade Three. And he had flat feet.'

The boys all hooted, competing in the amount of noise they could make.

'And his sausages are the best in Cobchester,' Gordon added.

'Are *you* made of best sausage, Porky?' asked Doug Staples, the wit of the group. Everyone laughed again. For although Mr. Dobbs the pork-butcher was a little thin man, his son at twelve was large, with small eyes in a broad pink face and with fat limbs. His outsize short trousers had to be specially made for him.

He was the sort of boy who was bound to be tormented at a tough council school in a tough district. And the area round Camellia Hill—known as the Jungle, because most of its sooty tangled streets were named after tropical flowers—was one of the toughest in the tough northern city of Cobchester.

Mrs. Dobbs had a shrewd idea of what went on, and came for Gordon most days after school. But today, the last before the Easter holiday, school had ended early and she hadn't been able to get away from the shop. Gordon had tried to slip out through the back gate, but he hadn't been quick enough. Now, in the quiet passageway behind the school, he was surrounded by a ring of boys, determined to have their fun.

He made a dash to break through the ring, but Tim Ridgeway planted himself in the way.

'Oh no, you don't, Porky Dobbs!' he said. 'We haven't finished with you yet.' He flicked Gordon's tie out. Gordon pushed it back and someone else flicked it out again.

'You're going to apologize!' said Tim.

'Apologize for what? I haven't done anything.'

'Apologize for your dad selling sawdust-and-dead-dog sausages.'

'I tell you he doesn't!' said Gordon, his voice rising and his face going redder.

But they were out to humiliate him. The excuse for it didn't matter.

'Temper, temper!' said Alan.

'Come on, now,' ordered Tim. 'Say it after me. The sooner

2

you say it, the sooner you'll get away. Say, "I apologize for my dad's rotten stuff." '

'But I don't!' yelled Gordon. 'I don't! It's not rotten!'

'Don't you shout at me!' said Tim. 'Say it, Porky Dobbs. Say it. *Say it*!'

Alan was the leader of the gang, but Tim was best at bullying. He caught Gordon by the wrist, intending to twist it. Goaded beyond bearing, Gordon lashed out and hit him on the chest. It was a light glancing blow which couldn't have hurt him, but two or three boys seized Gordon and held him back.

'So, you want to get tough, eh?' said Tim. 'Let him go, lads. You want a fight, Porky, eh? All right, you just hit me again.'

Gordon did nothing. He was on the point of breaking down.

'You're not afraid, are you, Porky?' Tim taunted him.

Still Gordon did nothing.

'Go on, hit me again!'

Desperately, Gordon threw himself at Tim, both fists whirling. For a moment it looked as though there'd be a fight. Tim stepped back and flicked a couple of blows at Gordon's face. Gordon collapsed, crying, with blood coming from his nose. Tim grabbed him by the collar and pulled him upright, ready to continue the humiliation. Then somebody called,

'Look out, Tim, Tony Boyd!'

Tony Boyd was six feet tall. He didn't say a word to Tim. He just looked at him.

'It's nothing to do with you!' declared Tim. 'Go back to church and play that organ!' But he let Gordon go, all the same.

Tony was just seventeen. He'd been born and bred in the Jungle, but he'd won a scholarship at eleven and gone to the grammar-school, a couple of miles out along the Wigan road. Now his parents had moved from the district, but Tony often came back. He was deputy organist at St. Jude's Church, and secretary of the youth club, and a frequent visitor to the Vicar, Mr. Wallace.

Nobody in the Jungle knew quite what to make of Tony. He was looked down on to some extent for being still at school at an age when most lads had long been earning wages. And he was distrusted by some because of his connexion with the church. But he was respected, too. Tony could use his fists, and his long bony arms and legs gave him plenty of speed and reach. He'd once (though losing his glasses and getting a black eye) beaten Alan Manning's big brother Jack in a fight that was well remembered in the Jungle.

'It's time you learned to mind your own flipping business!' Tim told him. 'You don't know what's happened. You're just interfering, as usual.'

'I can see young Gordon's had enough,' said Tony. 'Leave him alone now.'

The gang, all together, could have made short work of Tony if they'd tried. But nobody would make the first move, and Tim knew it as well as Tony did. In any case, the pleasure of bullying Porky Dobbs was clearly over. The atmosphere had been spoiled.

Tim spat.

'You wait till Rod sees you!' he said. Rod was Tim's elder brother. 'You didn't know Rod had been demobbed, did you? I'll tell him you've been on to me, and you can watch out then, Churchy Boyd. He'll break you in little bits and drop them all the way down Hibiscus Street. Come on, lads, we're not listening to him any more.'

The boys, led by Alan, were moving away already. Tim joined them, putting on a swagger so as not to look defeated.

'Going home, Gordon?' Tony asked.

Gordon's nose had stopped bleeding. He put his handkerchief away, and nodded.

'You live down at the bottom of Hibiscus Street, don't you?' said Tony. 'At Mr. Dobbs's?'

'Yes, we live over the shop.'

'I'm going partly the same way. I'll come with you. What was all that about?'

'Oh, nothing new. They're always on to me if they get me on my own.' The words made Gordon feel sorry for himself. 'I can't help it,' he said. 'I mean I can't help it if my dad's doing well and has a big shop. He makes the best things he can, with all the shortages. And I can't help being—you know.' Gordon could never bring himself to admit in so many words that he was fat.

Tony was thoughtful.

'Who do you play with, Gordon?'

'I don't play with anybody much.'

'What do you do at nights and weekends?'

'Read comics. Listen to the radio. Sundays my dad sometimes takes us out in the van.'

'It doesn't sound much of a life,' said Tony.

'It isn't,' said Gordon. He felt even sorrier for himself. 'I wish we could go somewhere else, where folks'd be nicer. My mum wishes that, too. The Jungle isn't what she's used to, you know. She says so, often. But of course we're tied to dad's shop.'

'I turn off here for the Vicarage. You'll be all right now, won't you, Gordon? Those lads went the other way. I don't think you'll see them again this afternoon.'

'Oh, I'll be all right,' said Gordon. He watched Tony's disappearing back for a moment, then trudged on. The conversation hadn't cheered him up. He still felt angry and ashamed. True, Tim Ridgeway and the lads hadn't made him say what they wanted about his dad. That was something. But he'd been reminded yet again that he was on his own, that years and years stretched ahead of him in which he'd be watching out at every corner in case Tim or some other bully should be around. Or else he'd be sitting at home, reading and listening and munching sweets. . . . As Tony had said, it wasn't much of a life.

The thought of sweets reminded him that he had money and coupons, and there was a shop at the next corner. He bought a stick of toffee and some paradise fruits and sat on a low wall near by to eat them.

He was safe now, because he only had to walk straight down Hibiscus Street, and it was the main shopping street of the Jungle, always busy. Nobody could harm you in Hibiscus Street in broad daylight. But he wasn't too keen to go home just yet. His mother might see that his nose had been bleeding, and she'd certainly notice a bruise on his cheek. And then she'd fuss.

Gordon took out his handkerchief, spat on it, and rubbed at a blood stain on his jacket. Then he became aware that a small child had sat down on the wall beside him and was talking in an undemanding way, half to herself. He knew her. Sheila something, that was her name. A kid of eight or nine. She went to his school.

'I saw you with Tony Boyd just now,' she was saying. 'He's nice, isn't he? He's ever so nice. He's my best friend.'

Gordon snorted with contempt and said nothing.

'Is he a friend of yours, too? If he is, you're lucky. I should think *everyone* would like Tony Boyd for their friend.'

At least she didn't seem to need any reply. Gordon put the last of the toffee stick in his mouth, threw the paper down, and groped in his pocket for the bag of paradise fruits.

'Specially since he won that great big prize,' said Sheila.

The remark caught Gordon's interest.

'What great big prize?' he asked.

She seemed surprised to be interrupted.

'I—I— I don't know . . .' she began doubtfully.

Gordon stared at her. She was a little thin slip of a thing, weighing perhaps half of what he weighed. She had longish straight fair hair, not too clean, and big wide grey eyes. She smiled uncertainly, then seemed suddenly to get into her stride.

'Why, Tony won a great big prize for playing the organ,' she said. 'All the best organ-players were there. They all tried. They played their organs till they—till they nearly burst. And Tony played best.'

'I never heard anything about it,' said Gordon.

'Well, they did. And famous people were there. The King was there.'

'Don't be daft, he wasn't.'

'He was. He was there. The King and the Queen and Princess Elizabeth. And Princess Margaret. They were all there.'

'Get away. And where was all this?'

'It was in a . . . in a . . .' Sheila hesitated. 'It was in a great big beautiful hall in London, like a cathedral. I went to see it. It was lovely.'

There was something in her look and her voice that almost made him believe her. Then he turned away. His eyes wandered round the black crumbling brickwork of this corner of the Jungle—in the foreground the small shabby shops of Hibiscus Street, and behind them the rows of squat terrace houses stretching down from here to the North-west Junction Canal. It was the only world he knew, and he was pretty sure it was the only world Sheila knew, too.

'You want your head examined,' he said.

Sneaking into his mind came the urge to get his own back. He gripped her small thin wrist.

'You're telling lies,' he said. 'Don't you know you shouldn't tell lies?'

She stared at him innocently from the wide grey eyes.

'I'm not,' she said. 'It happened. It did. The audience clapped and cheered and clapped and cheered, and the King stood up and put his crown on and said, "I award the prize to Tony!"'

Gordon started to twist her wrist. He felt shame and satisfaction all at once. She hadn't any right to make up such stories.

Sheila winced.

'What are you doing that for?' she asked.

'I'm doing it to teach you. To teach you to tell the truth.'

He twisted her wrist again. She was hurt and cried out.

'That was lies,' said Gordon. 'About Tony and the King and all that.' He remembered something from the recent bullying he'd suffered. 'Apologize. Say, "I apologize for telling rotten lies." '

She didn't seem to understand.

'The sooner you apologize, the sooner I'll let you go,' said Gordon. He felt a kind of triumph, a kind of satisfaction because the boys had tried to make him say what wasn't true but he was trying to make this kid say what *was* true.

'Go on. Say, "I apologize for telling rotten lies." '

She was whimpering a little, but still seemed not to be really there, seemed to be partly in a world of her own. He twisted her wrist a third time, more sharply. Now she came to earth and broke into sobs.

'I never thought,' she said, 'I never thought you'd be like that.'

When she started weeping, Gordon was ashamed. He stood back and let her go, looking at the red marks on her wrist.

'You're nasty,' she said. 'You're fat and nasty. I thought you'd be nice, because you were with Tony Boyd. And I was going to tell you something.'

'You haven't anything to tell.'

'I have. It's important.'

'You haven't. You couldn't have. You're a little daft kid. You don't know anything except silly nonsense.'

'If you knew what it was, you'd want to know.'

'Well, tell me,' said Gordon scornfully, 'then I'll know whether I want to know or not.'

'All right,' said Sheila. She leaned closer to him and whispered, though there was no one near. 'You saw the house that Tony went to?'

'The Vicarage? Yes.'

'It's *the pirate's house.*'

Gordon jeered.

'More tales!' he said. 'Pirate's house? Oh yes, very likely, I don't think! And I suppose the King lives next door?'

Sheila was shocked.

'Oh, no,' she said. 'The King lives at Buckingham Palace. I thought everybody knew that. But the house where Tony goes is the pirate's house.'

'You're barmy,' said Gordon. 'It's the Vicarage. Mr. Wallace lives there. He's a Vicar, not a pirate. There aren't any pirates now.'

'It isn't the Vicar that's the pirate,' Sheila said. 'It was years and years ago. Years and years and years ago. The man that lived there was a pirate, and he sailed the seven seas, all seven of them. And made people walk the plank. And brought back treasure. Topazes and cinnamon and gold moidores.'

'Cinnamon isn't treasure.'

'It is. It must be, it's in a poem. He captured the treasure from a stately Spanish galleon.'

'And buried it in the back-yard, I suppose,' said Gordon.

'Well, he must have buried it *somewhere,*' said Sheila, 'because he was a proper pirate, and pirates do.'

Gordon was going to laugh again, but the laugh died out as he looked into her eyes. She was perfectly serious. Again for a moment he almost believed her. But he looked away, and at once he knew it was nonsense.

'You want to wake up,' he said. 'What with the King giving prizes to Tony Boyd, and treasure in the Vicarage back-yard.'

'I didn't say there was treasure in the Vicarage back-yard!'

'Well, you said it was a pirate's house.'

'So it was. But I didn't say the treasure was in the back-yard. He might have put it anywhere. I expect there was a map. I mean, I expect there was a treasure map besides the ordinary map that I've got already. You see, when they'd buried the treasure they used to draw a special map with the place marked with a cross and directions for finding it. Like, "walk thirty paces north, then turn left towards Spyglass Hill" . . .'

'You said you've got a map yourself?'

'Yes. A map for finding the island. But I haven't got a treasure map.'

Gordon put a couple of paradise fruits in his mouth.

'Go on,' he said, sighing heavily. 'Tell me some more. Who gave you this map?'

'It was . . . it was . . .' Sheila hesitated a moment. Then, 'It was a mysterious stranger.'

Gordon laughed.

'With a black beard and a wooden leg?' he asked.

'Yes.'

'You ought to be put away,' said Gordon. 'Maps and mysterious strangers and the King giving prizes to Tony Boyd.

I never heard such rubbish.'

'It isn't rubbish,' she said, offended.

'It is. The King never gave Tony Boyd a prize.'

'He did . . . well, he might have done. You don't know that he didn't.'

'It'd have been in the local paper.'

'They might not have known.'

'And all this stuff about peg-legged pirates,' said Gordon.

'I can *prove* it about the pirate,' said Sheila with dignity. 'Come with me and I'll show you.'

'I can't be bothered.'

'Then don't call it lies.'

'All right, then, I believe you,' said Gordon, 'and now shut up about it.'

But she didn't want to shut up about it.

'The pirate carved his initials over the Vicarage front door,' she said. 'And an anchor, too. I expect it was a piratage in those days, not a vicarage.'

'And what were his initials?'

'C.C.'

'What does that stand for?'

'Captain Cutlass,' said Sheila promptly.

'Did the mysterious stranger tell you that?'

Again a moment's hesitation. Then,

'Yes, he did.'

'Have you asked Tony about it?'

'Oh, no,' Sheila was shocked. 'I couldn't do that. Tony's nearly grown up. He wouldn't have time. But I'll tell him if we find the treasure.'

'Who's "we"?' asked Gordon.

'I thought you might like to come and find it with me.'

'No, thank you, it's time I went for my tea.'

He moved away. She tagged along with him as he walked down Hibiscus Street towards Mr. Dobbs's shop.

'I don't mean just this minute,' she said. 'We could start to-morrow.'

'Listen,' said Gordon. 'There isn't any treasure. It's all a tale, like the King giving Tony a prize, and the man with the wooden leg.'

'It isn't a tale. The Vicarage was a pirate's house, and Captain Cutlass was a pirate, and where there's a pirate there's treasure. That's what pirates were *for,* burying treasure.'

Gordon made an impatient noise and walked faster, but she kept up with him.

'I'll take you,' she said. 'I'll bring the map and take you to find the pirate's island.'

They were outside Mr. Dobbs's shop.

'This is where I live,' said Gordon. 'I'm going to have my tea now. Aren't you going for *your* tea?'

She seemed vague about that.

'I might,' she said. 'I had school dinner.'

'That doesn't stop you wanting your tea, does it?'

'Well, I . . . I'm not bothered.'

Food was always an interesting subject to Gordon.

'I'm always ready for mine,' he said. 'And my breakfast, and my dinner, and my supper.'

He looked at her curiously. She was certainly thin.

'Doesn't your mum *give* you any tea?' he asked.

Sheila seemed uneasy with the subject. She wanted to get back to treasure.

'Come with me and find the island,' she said. 'Tomorrow morning.'

'I'm going to my grandma's tomorrow for Easter,' said Gordon. 'We won't be back until Monday night. And anyway I don't play with little kids like you.'

Then, reflecting that he hadn't anyone else to play with, he went on,

'Well, I might. You can call on Tuesday morning if you like, and see.'

He stuffed as many as he could of the paradise fruits into his mouth. There were two or three left in the bag. He put them in Sheila's hand.

'Here you are,' he said. 'You can have them. I'm going in now.' He chewed and swallowed. 'I want my tea.'

CHAPTER 2

'Gordon, who was that little lass you were with?' asked Mrs. Dobbs.

'Sheila.'

'Sheila who?'

'Oh, I don't know. She goes to my school. Woodrow, I think.'

'I didn't like the look of her. That frock. It's in holes.'

'Is it?' said Gordon without interest.

'If you ask me, she looks *poor*.'

'It's mostly poor people that live round here,' said Gordon.

'I don't know why you can't mix with *nice* children.'

Gordon had heard this before. By *nice* his mother meant well-dressed.

'Because there aren't any,' he said.

'There are, if only you'd seek them out. Anyway, never mind now. Tell me what you want for your tea. Beans, scrambled eggs, sausages?'

Gordon winced at the mention of sausages. Not that there was anything wrong with his dad's sausages, but the lads were always going on about them. His mother looked at him fondly, then stepped forward in alarm.

'Gordon!' she cried. 'What have you done to your nose?'

'It bled a bit,' he said.

'It looks to me as if someone had hit it. And that bruise. Gordon, are you all right?'

"Course I'm all right.'

'Is it those lads again?'

Gordon said nothing.

'It is! I know it is! Sidney! Sidney!'

Mrs. Dobbs went to the door that led from the living-room into the shop. Her husband came to meet her. He was a small, thin, grey-faced man who ate little and worried a lot. Gordon wasn't at all like him. Gordon took after his mother. Elsie Dobbs was plump, round-faced and rosy-cheeked. She'd been a pretty girl in her time, but was fond of her meals and fond of chocolate and cakes in between them, too.

'Sidney, those lads have been at him again,' she said. 'His nose! And a cut lip and a bruise coming up on his cheek. What did they do, Gordon love?'

'Nothing. I fell,' said Gordon. He didn't specially want to keep the boys out of trouble, but he knew that if his mother interfered it would only make things worse.

'You didn't do that by falling!' said Mrs. Dobbs. 'Oh, Gordon love, did they hurt you badly?'

'If he says he fell,' said Mr. Dobbs, 'I expect he fell.' He turned as if to go back into the shop.

'Sidney Dobbs!' cried his wife, her voice rising. 'Don't you *care*? Can't you stay at least and find out what happened to your son?'

'There's only young Alice in the shop,' said Mr. Dobbs.

'Shop? Shop? Can't you think of anything but the shop?'

'The shop keeps us all, doesn't it?' said Mr. Dobbs.

Mrs. Dobbs, with an air of great restraint, said nothing.

'And don't start telling me about how you weren't brought up to shopkeeping,' said Mr. Dobbs, 'because I've heard it all before.'

'I wasn't going to.'

'You were. I could see it in your eye.'

'Can I have my tea, Mum?' asked Gordon. He knew by heart the argument that was looming up, and he wanted to prevent it.

Mrs. Dobbs switched her attention at once.

'Of course you can, love,' she said. 'I'm sorry, I was forgetting. I hope your appetite's all right, after what you've been through. I'll do you two eggs, shall I, and a tin of beans? You just go and sit down till it's ready. You need a rest.'

Gordon went thankfully into the other room and put the radio on.

'The way you fuss over that lad . . .' said Mr. Dobbs.

'It's as well somebody bothers about him. You don't care, do you? They could kill him before you'd say anything.'

'Lads get into a rough-and-tumble now and again,' said Mr. Dobbs.

'Stick up for everybody before your own son, that's you.'

'I'm not sticking up for anyone. I'm just telling you.'

'And I'm telling you I shall see that headmaster about it after the holidays.'

'It won't make any difference.'

'I can't think,' Mrs. Dobbs said, 'why we don't take him away from the council school and send him somewhere nice.'

'Because he didn't get his scholarship,' said Mr. Dobbs, 'and until that new scheme they keep talking about comes in, that's an end of the matter.'

'It wouldn't be the end of the matter for a father who had a bit of push. There are schools where you pay.'

'Yes, like the one with the fancy uniform, up in Claypits. You think I'm going to spend good money to send a lad there? Well, I'm not. And listen here, Elsie, Gordon's not clever. He gets cosseted enough at home, without having him cosseted at school as well. He'll have to learn to stand on his own feet. . . . Hey, are you cooking for a blinking army?'

'The lad's got to keep his strength up.'

'He's overweight.'

'Overweight? He's well nourished, thanks to his mother,' said Mrs. Dobbs. 'I suppose you'd like him to be a skinny little thing?'

'Like me, eh? I know what you mean, even when you don't say it. Oh well, he won't starve tonight, any road. And now do you mind if I get back into the shop? You can't trust these young assistants.'

'Go on, I'm not stopping you,' said his wife. She turned the scrambled eggs out of the pan.

'Gordon!' she called.

'Yes, Mum.'

'It's ready. Your tea's ready, love. Come and enjoy it while it's hot.'

She sat beside her son as he ate. It always gave her pleasure to see him tucking into a good meal.

'I ought to complain about those lads,' she remarked when he'd finished.

'I don't want you to, Mum.'

'All right, we'll let it pass this time. But they'd better not touch you again or there'll be trouble. If I was you I'd keep well away from them. You're safest at home, and that's a fact. . . . What was it about, anyway?'

'Oh, only about dad. You know, not being in the war, and doing well in business and so on.'

'Well, that's not his fault,' said Mrs. Dobbs. And then, after a minute,

'All the same, I might have known it'd be something to do with him.'

CHAPTER 3

Mrs. Dobbs opened the side door on the Tuesday morning after Easter and frowned slightly at the small thin dirty figure outside.

'You just wait there a minute,' she said, and then,

'Gordon! There's that little lass at the door. You don't want to play with her, do you?'

Gordon almost said he didn't. But a bit of stubbornness, and some curiosity about Sheila's stories, prevented him.

'I might,' he said.

Mrs. Dobbs sighed. She had a mental image—fading a little by now—of beautifully neat, well-spoken children who'd be brought in cars to call for her son. But they never came, and he did need someone to play with.

'All right,' she said. 'Get some warm things on. It's nippy this morning. Keep out of the way of those lads. And don't be late for your dinner. Had you better have a hot drink before you go out?'

'I've only just had my breakfast.'

'Well, you can't be too careful, with that chest of yours.'

Mrs. Dobbs was convinced that Gordon had a weak chest, though the doctor wouldn't hear of it.

'I'll give you a spoonful of emulsion,' she said. 'Now go get your pullover and your thick stockings.'

She went back to the door. Sheila was sitting quietly on the step. She had on the same thin cotton frock as before, and sandals on her bare feet. Though she found it hard to think beyond her son, Mrs. Dobbs was not an unkind woman.

'You'd better come in,' she said reluctantly.

Sheila stepped inside.

'And where do you live, duck?'

Sheila didn't answer.

'You must know where you live,' said Mrs. Dobbs.

Sheila looked down and twisted her hands together.

'Come on now, you've got a tongue in your head, haven't you?'

'I live at Coral Court,' said Sheila suddenly.

'Coral Court? Where's that?'

'It's—it's a long way out, along the Wigan Road.'

'I never heard of it.'

'Oh, it's lovely. It has gardens all round. And trees. And fountains playing. And a lovely paved courtyard, all pink and white. That's why they call it Coral Court.'

'Well!' said Mrs. Dobbs. She sounded surprised but not un-believing. 'I suppose it's new, I've never seen it.' She looked Sheila up and down.

'You must have come out without your mum seeing you,' she said. 'I'm sure she can't know you're wearing that frock. And you ought to be well wrapped up, a day like this. Hadn't you better go home and get some warm clothes on?'

Sheila said nothing.

'What does your dad do?' asked Mrs. Dobbs. She was still trying to weigh up Sheila's suitability as a playmate for Gordon.

'He's at sea.' Sheila was silent for a moment, then said,

'He's a ship's captain.'

'Goodness.'

'Not a big ship like the *Queen Mary*,' Sheila said. 'A tramp steamer. Trading in the South Seas. For pearls and copra.'

'What's copra?'

'I don't know. They buy it from the South Sea Islanders. And I have a ship's cat that he gave me to remember him by, while he's away at sea. A white Persian ship's cat, called Shippy.'

'A *white Persian* ship's cat?' Mrs. Dobbs was suspicious now. 'Are you quite sure you're not telling me stories?'

''Course she's telling stories,' said Gordon, coming back dressed for out-of-doors. 'She tells stories all the time. She said the King gave a prize to Tony Boyd.'

Both Dobbses, mother and son, stared at Sheila. She looked back at them innocently.

'Well, come on, if we're going,' said Gordon. And, when the door had closed behind them, 'anyway, where *are* we going?'

'To find the pirate's island. I'll show you his house first.'

'You mean the Vicarage? I've seen it. Hundreds of times.'

'I want to show you his initials. And his anchor. And then I'll show you the map for finding the island.'

'The one the black-bearded man with the wooden leg gave you?'

'Yes.'

'Come on, then,' said Gordon, a little impressed in spite of himself.

They walked up Hibiscus Street and turned into Azalea Place, where the Vicarage stood. It was a square old building and had a fanlight over its front door, which opened straight on to the street. It all looked very run-down, smoke-blackened and shabby, and it was hemmed in on both sides by tumbledown terrace dwellings.

'Look on top of the door,' said Sheila. 'Look carefully.'

Gordon peered. Above the fanlight, a piece of carved and lettered stone was set into the brickwork. It was as sooty as the rest of the building, and the lettering had been partly worn away, so you could only just make it out.

'It says "C.C., 1795", and there's an anchor carved underneath it,' said Sheila. 'And ships had anchors, and pirates had ships, and 1795 was pirate days, so that *proves* it was a pirate's house.'

She was triumphant. Gordon puzzled out the lettering. It was just as she'd said, and the shape underneath it did look rather like an anchor. Again he was impressed in spite of himself.

'Go on,' he said. 'Now show me the map.'

She drew a piece of paper from her knicker-leg and unfolded it. It was tattered and smudged with fingerprints.

'Is that supposed to be a pirate map?' asked Gordon. 'It looks like a sheet out of an old notebook. A pirate map would be on parchment, all yellowy and crumbling at the edges.'

'I never said it was a pirate map.'

'You said a man with a wooden leg gave it you.'

'Yes, well . . . well, it wasn't the pirate himself. He said the pirate was his grandpa. This is only a copy. He copied it from the real map.'

'Let's have a look.'

It was indeed a map, roughly drawn in pencil on the ruled paper. One or two place-names were written in what looked like a grown-up hand.

'Vicarage—Camellia Hill—Wigan Road—Midwell Street,' read Gordon. 'And a great big question-mark. And "Island in River Midwell". What does it all mean?'

'Miss Herrick said . . .' began Sheila, then stopped and started again. 'The man with the black beard told me the pirate had an island. In the middle of the River Midwell. So I expect that was where he buried his treasure.'

'There aren't any islands in the middle of rivers anywhere round here,' said Gordon. 'There aren't any rivers either, for that matter.' Then he looked up to see that someone was beckoning to them from a window of the Vicarage.

'That's Mr. Wallace,' said Sheila. 'Look, he wants us to go in.'

'You seem to know him.'

'Of course I know him. Because of Tony I know him. He's nice.'

The door under the fanlight opened. Mr. Wallace, the Vicar, appeared. He was a well-built middle-aged man in horn-rimmed spectacles, and he was wearing a roll-necked sweater. Gordon knew that a lot of people didn't approve of the Vicar, and one of the reasons was that he hardly ever wore a clerical collar except on Sundays. Another reason was that he often mixed with the roughest characters in the Jungle. And yet another was that he'd been known to go into local pubs. It was even whispered that he'd been seen with a pint of beer in his hand.

'Hullo, Sheila,' he said. 'Come in. My wife's got something for you. Hullo, young fellow. Goodness, you're a hefty one, aren't you? . . . Along that way, Sheila, you know where the kitchen is. I'll be with you in a minute. Just let me get to know your friend.'

Two rooms opened left and right from the hallway, and a passage ran towards the back of the house. Sheila went along the passage. Mr. Wallace opened the door on the left and took Gordon into an extremely shabby room in which stood a rolltop desk, open and brimming with papers.

'My study, so-called,' he said. 'Now, lad, I'm glad to meet you. You must be Gordon Dobbs.'

Gordon nodded, surprised.

'I thought so when I saw you out there just now. Tony Boyd was talking to me about you the other night. I know more than you think. It's a good shop, Dobbs's. Folk are jealous, of course, and youngsters pick it up from older ones, unfortunately.... Can you box, Gordon?'

Mr. Wallace put up his fists. Gordon didn't respond. Mr. Wallace pretended to hit him a series of blows on face and chest.

'You're a biggish target,' he said. 'Why don't you join Tony's club? Learn a bit of self-defence.'

'I don't care for fighting,' said Gordon.

'All right, lad, fair enough. I'm not trying to persuade you. It was just a thought, that's all. Anyway, I'm glad to see Sheila's got a bit of company today. A remarkable child, but too much on her own.'

Gordon started. Sheila didn't seem all that remarkable to him —except that she told surprising tales. But perhaps that was what Mr. Wallace meant.

'We all try to help her,' the Vicar said. 'Her teacher, and Jill What's-her-name at the library, and Tony—and ourselves, of course. But she's a worry to us. No telling what will happen next.'

'She's not barmy, is she?' asked Gordon, puzzled.

'Oh no no, far from it. I didn't mean that at all. She's an imaginative, sensitive child in a very difficult situation.... Have you been to her home, Gordon? No? I thought not. Well, don't be too surprised if you're not encouraged.... Now, I expect my wife will have got that little package ready for her by now. Let's go along and see.'

Gordon followed him along the passage to the big, quarry-tiled Vicarage kitchen. It was dark and old-fashioned, and Mrs. Wallace worked in it alone. The last maid had gone off to war work in 1940, and there was never likely to be another.

Sheila had a paper-wrapped parcel, and she pushed it instinctively out of sight behind her back as Gordon went in.

'I'll see what I can do about that other thing,' Mrs. Wallace was telling her. 'You must come again in a day or two.'

Freda Wallace was a tall, gaunt and harassed-looking woman.

She was thought to be stand-offish, and her accent was out of place in the Jungle. In spite of frequent, abrupt kindnesses, she was more disliked than liked. Gordon had seen her a few times in the shop. He was just a bit afraid of her. But he was also curious. And on this unusual morning he felt bold enough to put a question.

'Who was "C.C."?' he asked.

The Vicar and Mrs. Wallace looked at each other for a moment as if they didn't see what he was getting at. Then the Vicar understood.

'You mean the person whose initials are over the door?' he said. 'I don't know, Gordon. This house didn't come into the Church's hands until about eighty years ago. I've no idea who had it before then. I suppose we could find out if we tried. But I'm not much given to rooting about in the past, to tell you the truth. I find the present quite enough to cope with.'

He thought for a moment and added,

'There are probably all kinds of clues in that attic. There's the junk of ages up there. You must look at it some day.'

'Oh, could we?' asked Sheila, her face lighting up.

Mrs. Wallace didn't seem too pleased by the idea.

'I suppose you can some time,' she said. 'Not just yet. We're so busy at present. And this house is a lot to manage, without turning the attics out.'

Then there was a change in her expression and she spoke to her husband.

'Some of the things up there might be worth something, Harry,' she said. 'And we could use a little money just now, for you-know-what.'

'So we could,' said the Vicar. 'So we could.'

Gordon stuck doggedly to his subject.

'Could "C.C." have been a pirate?' he asked.

'A pirate?' Mr. Wallace smiled. 'Well, that's an exciting thought. I've never heard anything of the sort myself. But you never know, do you? Let's say—let's say it's hardly an odds-on chance but it's not totally beyond the bounds of possibility.'

'What did he mean by that?' Gordon asked Sheila when they were out in the street again.

'He meant "very likely",' said Sheila.

CHAPTER 4

'Well, what do we do now?' asked Gordon.

'We go and look for the River Midwell. And then we look for the pirate's island. That's what I brought the map for. But first I've got to take something somewhere.'

'I'll come with you.'

'You can come part of the way.'

They walked up Camellia Hill and turned eastward along the Wigan Road, towards the city centre. Soon the road crossed over the railway.

'You wait for me here,' said Sheila when they were on the railway bridge. 'Don't go away. I shan't be long.'

'Why can't I come?'

'Because you can't. And you haven't to watch where I go. Look the other way.'

Gordon opened his mouth to argue, then closed it and did as he was told, looking back the way they'd come. But after a few moments he turned, just in time to see her disappear downhill into Slaughter Street. That was the way to the

Shambles. Gordon was puzzled. The Shambles was the worst corner of the whole Jungle. Nobody went down there who could help it. But he wasn't a boy to spend much time guessing, and just then a train went under the bridge and drew his attention away.

The land sloped sharply down from here towards the canal, and after passing beneath his feet the train soon rumbled out on to the viaduct which took it across the water. Under and alongside the viaduct at this side of the canal was a big goods yard, and for several minutes Gordon watched from the bridge as small steam-engine fussed around, shunting trucks. Then he began to get bored. There was no sign of Sheila. He walked along the main road to the top of Slaughter Street to see if she was coming, but she wasn't.

To Gordon the world beyond his doorstep was on the whole hostile. He felt fairly safe on the main roads, though he didn't often to go so far from home as this. But he was wary about side streets. And he didn't like the look of Slaughter Street at all. It was lined on both sides with dingy tumbledown houses. In a place like this Gordon felt himself to be a natural quarry for any gang of lads that might be about. And he hadn't the speed to get away if they came after him.

Sheila still wasn't in sight, but a hundred yards or so down the street on the left he could see a sweetshop. As usual Gordon had money and sweet-coupons. It felt a long time now since breakfast, and there wasn't anyone to be seen in Slaughter Street. He ran quickly down to the shop, bought some chocolate, and lingered inside for quite a while, confident that he'd see Sheila through the glass door if she went past. Then it struck him that she might return a different way to the railway bridge, and he'd better go back there in case she was waiting for him. And as soon as he left the shop he walked almost into the arms of Tim Ridgeway, one of the boys who'd been bullying him a few days earlier.

Tim was on his own, kicking a stone along the pavement. Gordon tried to walk past him but had no luck. Tim's eyes lit up.

'It's my old pal Porky!' he said with delight. 'How do, Porky?' And he flicked Gordon's tie out.

Gordon still tried with dignity to walk on, but Tim wouldn't let him.

'I spoke to you, Porky Dobbs,' he said. 'I said "How do?"'

Don't you answer when your pals speak to you?'

'Hullo,' said Gordon.

Tim looked at him narrow-eyed, searching for some grounds for a quarrel. Though not the biggest or toughest of the boys, he was the most unpleasant—the one Gordon would least have wished to meet.

'Get out of my way,' Tim said.

Gordon stepped aside.

Tim changed direction.

'You're still in the way,' he said.

Gordon moved again. Tim grinned, satisfied that he'd found a sufficient cause for trouble, and pushed him in the chest.

'You just stop obstructing people,' he said.

A sudden grim determination came to Gordon. Tim was used to shoving him around, especially when the gang was there. But today Tim was on his own, and Gordon was bigger and heavier. He moved in, surprising Tim, who hadn't expected any resistance. Gordon clasped him in a bear-hug. Tim kicked and wriggled violently. Gordon hung on, then leaned forward, using his weight to force Tim down. Before either of them knew what was happening, they were in the gutter with Gordon on top, still grimly pinning Tim's arms but getting his shins kicked by Tim's boots.

Then Gordon's determination was followed by anger. He banged Tim's head on the roadway. Tim yelled with pain and stopped kicking. Gordon banged his head again.

'Here, are you trying to kill him?' demanded a man in cap and muffler who'd just come round the corner. 'Stop it. Hey, stop it!'

Gordon stood up. He felt deep satisfaction and found he was grinning. Tim, too, climbed to his feet, not really hurt, but furious with pain and humiliation.

'Our Rod's come back, Porky Dobbs!' he snarled. 'I'll have him on to you. He'll kill you, that's what he'll do.' And Tim stumped away.

Gordon looked after him, hardly able to believe that he'd won. Tim's threat worried him a little, because Rod had a bad reputation for violence, but he put it out of his mind.

'You ought to be ashamed of yourself, a big lad like you,' said the man in the cap and muffler. 'Can't you pick on somebody your own size?' But he moved on without waiting for Gordon to say anything. When Sheila arrived a minute later,

Gordon was sitting on a doorstep, rolling down his stockings to look at the red marks on his ankles but still half smiling to himself.

'A lad tried to push me around,' he said. 'But I showed him!'

'You're brave, Gordon,' said Sheila. There was just a hint in her voice of the tone in which she'd spoken about her hero Tony Boyd. Gordon was warmed and encouraged by it.

'They're always on to you, aren't they?' she said. 'But you're a match for them.' And then she seemed to slip away into her own world. 'Surrounded by foes but fearless,' she said, 'the schooner sailed the pirate-infested seas.' She looked around with far-off eyes, as if the streets of Cobchester were dissolving in her imagination into the endless grey ocean. 'The skipper kept a sharp lookout, ready to crowd on all sail and show the rogues a clean pair of heels. One he had beaten already in gallant hand-to-hand fight, but his wounds needed tending. . . . Here, Gordon, let me put a bit of spit on that ankle.'

She put her mouth to his sores, licking them with small moist tongue.

'I made Tim Ridgeway walk the plank, anyway,' said Gordon.

The name startled her.

'Tim?' she said. 'Oh, Gordon, I'm sorry.'

'It's not your fault, is it? It's nothing to do with you.'

'It's . . . well, no, it's not my fault, but . . .'

'He said he'd set Rod on to me,' said Gordon, and added with a touch of bravado, 'I'm not worried.'

'You don't want that. Keep away from Rod Ridgeway, Gordon. There's no telling what he might do.'

She was upset.

'Well,' said Gordon, humouring her, 'what distant shore do we set sail for now?'

Sheila seemed glad of the change of subject, but she'd been jolted out of her make-believe.

'I told you,' she said. 'We're off to find the River Midwell. This way, Gordon.'

CHAPTER 5

They crossed the Wigan Road and continued up Slaughter
Street, which led into a higher part of Camellia Hill. This
district was known as Claypits, and Upper Camellia Hill was
its busy main street. There were corner groceries and pubs and
pawnshops and loan offices, and hardware stores spilling on to
the pavement with tin baths and fenders and ornamental fire
irons. Higher still, the shops faded out and the road was less
busy, lined with houses and criss-crossed by narrow streets.
Here and there were bare cindery open spaces. If they turned
round they could now see below them the whole smoky tangle
of Claypits and the Jungle, sprawling downhill to the canal.

'Midwell Street,' said Sheila after they'd taken three or four
turnings. 'We're getting near.'

'There's no river round here,' said Gordon.

They pored over the little rough map. To Gordon it looked
even less convincing than it had done before. He couldn't
believe it was going to lead them anywhere.

'Your black-bearded peg-legged man must have got it wrong,' he said.

'He didn't. I know he didn't. Anyway, why's it called Midwell Street if there isn't a river? There must be one.'

'Who says there's a River Midwell anyway?' said Gordon. 'Only old Pegleg. I never heard of it before.'

'Well, we've come all this way. At least let's go and look.'

Half-way along Midwell Street they found it. On the northern side was a gap between two rows of houses. In the middle of the gap was a low parapeted wall, like one side of a bridge. Flanking it were a few feet of iron railings. Beyond them were tall grass, rushes, nettles. And there was the sound of water.

Two of the railings were bent bow-leggedly apart, where countless children had pushed a way through. Sheila slipped between them without thinking. Gordon, to his shame, got stuck. He puffed and panted, shoving away and getting red in the face, while Sheila tugged at the arm that was through. When at last he was at the other side of the railings, there was a big rust-mark on his jacket.

After half a dozen paces they realized why the area had been railed off. It was dangerous. Hidden by high weeds was a drop of ten or twelve feet, and at the foot of it was the muddy margin of the water. This was the River Midwell. Shallow and sluggish, it flowed towards them between two lines of back-yards. In and around it were oil drums, motor tyres, bits of old bicycles and prams and bedsteads, junk of every kind. A few small and very dirty children were paddling in the middle of it all.

Gordon and Sheila slithered down to the water's edge. And now they could see what became of the river at this point.

'There it goes,' said Sheila. 'Into a tunnel and under the road and you never see it again.'

The tunnel was big enough for them both to get into, and the water was only a few inches deep. But neither felt tempted by the dank blackness.

'There'll be rats in there,' said Gordon.

Sheila shuddered.

'Let's go back to the road.'

They made their way back to the gap in the railings. Gordon passed his jacket ahead of him and got through without much trouble, but at the cost of another rust-mark, this time on his pullover.

'Well,' he said, 'where do we go now? There isn't any island.

Unless it's farther up the stream.'

'No, it's lower down, I'm sure.'

'Pegleg told you so, eh?'

'Yes.'

'Well, it can't be in the middle of the tunnel. I never heard of an island in a tunnel.'

'Then we'd better look for the other end,' said Sheila. 'The river must come out somewhere.'

'Does the map show it?'

'No, there's just a question mark.'

'Old Pegleg wasn't very thorough,' said Gordon. 'He should have listened to what his grandpa the pirate told him. That is, if there ever was a Pegleg, never mind a grandpa.'

Sheila said nothing.

'Who *really* drew the map?' Gordon asked.

She still said nothing.

'Anyway, it must be getting on for dinner-time,' Gordon said. He looked with dismay at his rust-marked clothes. His shoes were wet and muddy, and his stockings were splashed. He wondered how he was going to face his mother. There'd be trouble when she saw the state he was in. Without exactly thinking about it, he decided to put off the moment of reckoning.

'All right,' he said, 'we'll go and look for the other end of the tunnel. I'm hungry, though. Aren't you?'

Sheila was still silent. Mealtimes didn't seem to mean much to her. But when he brought from his pocket the bar of chocolate he'd bought just before the encounter with Tim Ridgeway, he saw her eye on it and had the feeling that she was hungry too.

'Seeing I'm twice as big as you, I should have twice as much,' he said. But he broke the bar in the middle and gave her half. She ate her chocolate neatly, square by square. Then she was eager to move on.

'I think we'll have to go down Water Lane,' she said.

Water Lane was a long straight street that continued the line of the vanished River Midwell. It was Gordon who realized what had happened.

'The river used to flow down here before they covered it in,' he said. 'They built the street over the top of it.'

'Well, then, all we've got to do is follow the street,' said Sheila.

This part of Water Lane wasn't just tumbledown, it was almost derelict. Along it were empty sites where ancient houses had been pulled down and not replaced. There were junkyards, there was an old walled garden with nothing in it now but weeds. At one point was a curved row of tall, once-stylish houses with the name 'Riverside Crescent' still readable, but now it was only a crumbling tenement. You felt that nothing had been the same since the river went underground.

Farther down, after crossing the Wigan Road, Water Lane became livelier. There were people about, and motor-vehicles, and a few shops. The lane finished by making a T-junction with Wharf Street, where the North-west Junction Canal Company's headquarters were. Everything was bolted and barred now, for the company had closed down at the end of the war and the canal was disused. But facing the children as they reached Wharf Street was a yard with a painter's-and-decorator's sign over its entrance. At the far side of the yard was a ten-foot brick wall. And beyond that brick wall, they knew, was the canal.

A chalked notice beneath the painters' sign said: KEEP OUT. THIS MEANS YOU. The yard was empty except for a couple of parked vans, a locked wooden hut, and some equipment lying in a corner.

'Let's go in,' said Sheila. 'I want to look over that wall.'

'Can't you read the notice?' said Gordon, who liked to keep out of trouble.

'I don't care. There's nobody to stop us.'

'Anyway, you can't reach to see over the wall.'

'Let me stand on your shoulders.'

'You still couldn't reach,' said Gordon.

'Well, let's borrow that ladder in the corner.'

'We daren't. Somebody might come.'

'I'll watch out. You move it, Gordon, you're stronger.'

Gordon would have protested, but there was something compelling in Sheila's voice. She was in charge. It was her quest.

An unaccustomed feeling of recklessness came over him. On a day when he'd made such a mess of his jacket, a day when he was being deliberately late for his dinner, he felt capable of anything. Besides, the whole place seemed quiet. There probably wasn't much risk.

He dragged the ladder across the gravel—it was heavier than he'd thought—and made two or three attempts to rear it against the wall. Sheila left her lookout post and helped him. Soon it was in position. She scrambled up and sat perilously on top of the wall with her legs dangling on the far side. Gordon climbed up and stood near her, his feet still on the ladder. He felt slightly dizzy and gripped its sides hard. Immediately below him was the black canal water, looking as if it might suck him in.

To the right the canal was wide and formed a basin, round which were the empty wharves of the canal company. To the left was a dark canyon formed by the high warehouse walls which rose from both sides of the water. At the near side, and only a few yards away from him, was a small platform a few feet above surface level, with a flight of stone steps going down from it into the canal. And beside the platform was a tunnel— clearly the other end of the tunnel they'd already seen. Out of the tunnel and into the canal poured the water of the River Midwell.

'Well, there's your river!' said Gordon.

'I knew we'd find it,' Sheila said.

'But this is the end of it. It hasn't an island.'

'Wait a minute,' said Sheila. 'What's that over there? In the widest part of the canal.'

Gordon looked. Yes, there was something. And it was an island of a kind, though it didn't seem to be a natural one. It was a few square feet of weedy ground, edged with indigo brick-work which disappeared below the canal surface. Cemented into the brickwork at intervals were half a dozen stout iron rings, obviously meant for typing up barges, though now unused.

'It's something to do with the Canal Company,' he said. 'Part of the wharf system. It can't be what you're looking for, Sheila. It can't possibly.'

'Oh, it is!' she cried. 'It is, it is. It's the pirate's island!'

'Looks to me,' said Gordon, 'as if there's been a bridge connecting it to the main wharf. Just a footbridge. Maybe the island was only there as a support for the bridge. And now they've pulled the bridge down. It isn't from pirate times at all. Well, honestly, how could it be?'

But Sheila just gazed. The patch of barren ground and purple brick dissolved before her eyes into a green island fringed with osiers. Instead of the canal she saw the River Midwell, widening out to form a calm lake, glinting in the sun. It was a hundred and fifty years ago, and Camellia Hill was part of the English countryside, sloping gently down to the lake-shore. Just the place for a pirate to retire to. She pictured him, home at last from sailing the seas, sitting in his beautiful new house with his initials over the door. She saw him rowing out to the island, with a spade in the bottom of the boat and a small but very heavy oak chest. . . .

'Sheila! Come down!'

Gordon shouted to her. He was half-way down the ladder already. She slithered after him. For a man in overalls was just coming into the yard.

Gordon and Sheila darted to the nearest parked van and ducked behind it. It didn't seem as if the man had noticed them. But when he got to the middle of the area he saw the ladder up against the wall and walked over to it, puzzled. The children scurried from one van to another, nearer the way out. The man heard something, looked round, moved towards them.

'Go on, run!' urged Gordon.

Sheila raced to the gate and was away. Gordon lumbered after her. But he wasn't built for speed. The man chased him and caught him by the jacket collar, which tore.

'What were you up to?' he demanded. He was thin, middle-aged, with a tanned face and blue eyes. He looked good-natured, but he was cross.

'What were you doing with my ladder?'

'W-we wanted to look at the canal.'

'And what if you'd fallen in? That'd have been the end of you. And I'd have been blamed, most likely. I've a good mind to hand you over to the police.'

Gordon shuddered. He'd never had that threat made to him before.

A small figure sidled up.

'Well, and what do *you* want?' the man asked.

'Please, I was with him,' said Sheila.

'Oh, you were, were you?' The man hesitated. He didn't seem sure what to do. Then he made up his mind. 'Well, you come in here again, either of you, and you'll be in the Juvenile Court before you know what's happened. Now, little 'un, you get out. And as for you'—he glared at Gordon as fiercely as he could —'just see if you can be through that gate before I land my boot on your backside!'

Gordon, released, shot away faster than he'd ever moved in his life. The man grinned. He didn't like getting kids into trouble. And it was partly his own fault, he reflected. He shouldn't have left that ladder there. You couldn't have people risking life and limb on your premises, using your own property. He turned away, resolving to be more careful tomorrow, or anyway next week.

Outside in Water Lane, Gordon slowed down, his heart thumping. Sheila was waiting for him. He grinned. He'd won a fight and tracked a river and been caught trespassing and torn and dirtied his jacket, and it was long past dinner-time. There'd never been anything like it. Trouble with his mother loomed ahead. But in spite of that he felt unusually contented. He thought more highly of himself than he'd done a few hours ago.

'Quite a morning, wasn't it?' he said.

He could tell that Sheila was lost once more in her own world. Dirt and torn clothes and dinner-time meant little to her. She answered him as if from a distance.

'Lovely,' she said. 'Lovely. And it's only the beginning. You'll have to build one now.'

Gordon stared.

'Build one what?' he asked.

'Build a boat. Or a raft. Or whatever we're going to use to get to the island.'

CHAPTER 6

'It was that little lass that led him into it,' said Mrs. Dobbs.

Mr. Dobbs grunted, only half listening. He was making up the accounts.

'Tearing his jacket like that. He'd never have done it on his own.'

'Lads do tear their jackets,' said Mr. Dobbs.

'Our Gordon never used to,' said his wife. 'But he came home looking like a ragamuffin today. And late, hours late. It just shows, I always say. They get like the children they play with. If she comes here again I shall send her about her business.'

She turned towards Gordon, who was reading a comic in the corner of the room.

'You hear that, Gordon?' she said. 'You're not playing with that little lass any more. She's not suitable.'

'I don't *want* to play with her any more,' said Gordon. It seemed as if he was never going to hear the last of his torn and dirty clothes, and of the good dinner that Mrs. Dobbs said had been ruined (though he'd eaten it without noticing anything

32

wrong). It was Sheila who'd got him into this trouble. He'd had enough of her company.

But even as he said it, he felt disloyal, and he felt disloyal again next day when his mother told him she'd turned Sheila away from the door. And though he didn't believe Sheila's unlikely stories, he found he missed them. His curiosity had been stirred and wasn't satisfied.

Moreover, he began to get bored. Mrs. Dobbs spent a good part of the day helping her husband. Her attentions to Gordon, though intense, were not continuous. There were long stretches of time when he had nothing to do.

One of Sheila's remarks began to occupy his mind. She'd told him he must build a boat or raft to go to the island. She'd spoken as if it was easy, as if any boy could do it. Gordon knew that building a boat was far too difficult. But the thought of a raft appealed to him. And he remembered that in one of the outhouses in Mr. Dobbs's back-yard were the floorboards taken up last year from the spare room.

Gordon wasn't a maker. His father had never had the time or inclination for carpentry or for doing odd jobs about the house. Gordon hadn't been brought up in the way of such activities. But building a raft sounded fairly easy. And there was something special about it. It was exciting, it was a way of going to places. Not that he was much impressed by that sour patch of land that Sheila chose to call Pirate's Island, or that he had any clear idea in his mind of what he'd do with the raft when it was finished. He didn't think much about that. He just had a fancy to make a raft.

The outhouse that held the old floorboards also held a deal table, turned out from the kitchen some years ago. Gordon didn't ask if he could have it, because his parents, so unlike each other in most ways, were both inclined to hold on to old possessions in case they came in useful. But he was sure the table wouldn't be missed. And he felt that if he could nail nine or ten planks side by side across it and then turn the whole thing upside down he would have a well-designed and comfortable raft.

Mr. Dobbs kept his tools, such as they were, in a corner of the other, larger outhouse that served as a garage for the van. Gordon found a hammer and went to the corner ironmonger's for a pound of shining two-inch nails. Then he set to work. It wasn't as easy as he'd expected. Nails often bent instead of going in straight, and you had to try to get them out with pliers. Planks refused to stay still and be fixed to the table. After half an hour he'd only got two of the floorboards nailed, more or less straight and side by side, across the table top.

Gordon felt sticky and dirty and not much inclined for further effort just yet. But he was quite pleased with himself, all the same. At least he'd made a start. It occurred to him to go and report progress to Sheila. This of course was against his mother's instructions. It was also, though he didn't realize it himself, just what he'd intended to do all along.

Gordon didn't know where Sheila lived, but he remembered that the Vicar and Mrs. Wallace has seemed to know her quite well. He could call at the Vicarage and ask for her address. He helped himself to some biscuits from the tin in the kitchen and then walked cautiously up Hibiscus Street to Camellia Hill.

He looked as usual in the toyshop window, then at the comics on the racks outside Mr. Moult's, the newsagent's. Next beyond the newsagent's was the showroom of N. J. Batten, Antiques— better known in the Jungle as Nick Batten's junkshop. Old worm-eaten furniture, cracked mirrors, dark-brown paintings and china dogs, that was all you expected to see in Nick Batten's, and to Gordon it was hardly worth a second glance. But today his eye was caught by something out of the ordinary, prominently displayed in the window. It was a brass-bound wooden chest with a domed lid—just like the treasure-chest he'd seen in a film a few months before. It wasn't very big, only about eighteen inches long, but it would hold quite a lot of doubloons or pieces-of-eight. And neatly burned into its side it had the initials 'C.C.'

Gordon felt a flutter in the stomach. The chest fitted so perfectly into Sheila's fantasy, and its appearance in the window was so well timed, that it seemed uncanny. But of course it must be coincidence. He soon recovered from the shock. All the same, the urge to tell Sheila about it was overwhelming.

He turned into Azalea Place and went up to the Vicarage door. He hadn't been looking forward to this call, for he was slightly in awe of Mr. Wallace and rather more in awe of his wife. But with the chest filling his thoughts he forgot to be afraid and rang the bell confidently.

It was Mrs. Wallace who came, and she took a moment to recognize Gordon. But when she did, she was glad enough to hear that he was going to see Sheila.

34

'Ask her to call as soon as she can, will you?' she said. 'I've got something to give her.'

'Can I take it for you?' Gordon asked.

'I think not. No, I think not. Just ask her to call.'

Gordon wanted to talk about what he'd seen.

'I saw a chest in Nick Batten's window,' he said. 'Like a treasure-chest.'

'Oh?' Mrs. Wallace seemed startled.

'And it had "C.C." on the side. Just like over the door of this house.'

It was a moment before Mrs. Wallace spoke, and then there was a slight undertone of sharpness in her voice.

'If I were you,' she said, 'I wouldn't be inquisitive. Because it isn't really anything to do with you, is it?'

Gordon felt snubbed and went red.

'I'm sorry,' he said, though he couldn't see that he'd done anything wrong.

'It's quite all right. Now, you wanted Sheila's address. You'll find her at 17, The Shambles.' And Mrs. Wallace started closing the door. Gordon had just time to thank her before he found himself alone on the doorstep.

The Shambles.

That was as big a shock in its way as seeing the chest. People from outside looked on all this part of Cobchester as one large, poor district, but those inside it knew that there were many distinctions. Claypits considered itself a cut above the Jungle. Within the Jungle, the streets west of Hibiscus Street were reckoned superior to those farther east, and uphill was better than down. But everyone, east or west, uphill or down, looked askance at the Shambles. It was the inner citadel of slumdom.

It stood where the old slaughterhouse had been, near the railway sidings and the canal. A century earlier, animals had been brought by road, by railway truck, by barge, to be killed for food. Then the slaughterhouse had gone, and someone with an eye to business had packed the area with little cheap dwellings—built, it was said, mainly from the slaughterhouse rubble. There were legends of ghostly patches of blood, remaining for ever sticky. There were people who swore they'd heard the screams of long-dead animals, echoing down the years. There were tales of more recent violence—of people brutally attacked to be robbed of small sums of money. There were taller stories—of mysterious disappearances, of bodies weighted and thrown into the canal.

There was no disentangling truth from fiction. Probably most of the tales were made up. What was known was that police and rent collectors went into the Shambles in pairs for safety's sake. What was known was that the Shambles was at the top of the Corporation list for slum clearance, and but for the war would have been pulled down five years ago.

Gordon was horrified that Sheila should live in such a place. And yet there was a corner of his mind that wasn't entirely surprised. She'd romanced to his mother about her home. She hadn't let him come with her, or even see which way she went, but he knew she'd gone down Slaughter Street, and that led to the Shambles. The clues had been there, and he'd noticed them, though he hadn't wanted to draw conclusions.

He was now in half a mind to go home. His parents wouldn't want him to set foot down there. But the urge to tell Sheila of the raft, and still more of the chest in Nick Batten's window, was strong. And he had a duty to give her Mrs. Wallace's message.

Reluctantly he walked up to the Wigan Road, eastward over the railway bridge, and down towards the slaughterhouse wall. This was enemy territory again, though the memory of how he'd dealt with Tim Ridgeway gave him a little courage. Well down the street, set into the wall, was an archway, with a lamp above it and a narrow cobbled alley visible beyond.

Gordon hovered uneasily around the archway for two or three minutes. He was nervous about going into the Shambles, nervous about asking the way to Sheila's home. Than an old man shuffled out through the arch, placing his feet in front of him with difficulty. His head was well down and he was muttering something to himself. Gordon plucked up courage.

'Excuse me!' he said. But there was no response. He called out again, more loudly. There was still no answer.

'I want Number 17. Sheila Woodrow!' he shouted at the old man's back. The old man took no notice, perhaps didn't hear. But a woman's voice from somewhere in the shadows answered,

'Round to your left. Third entry.'

The street was narrow and nameless, for all addresses within the slaughterhouse walls were simply 'The Shambles'. Dwellings had been crammed in a tightly as possible, filling all corners and taking advantage of existing walls wherever they could. Entries ran in among the now-crumbling brick-work like holes into a warren. There were few people about, though a couple of large, slippered women filling buckets at an outdoor tap eyed Gordon with some curiosity.

The third entry led into a small, dark, stone-flagged lobby. Gordon stubbed his toe on a dustbin and disturbed a cat, which hissed at him. Then his eyes got used to the gloom, and he saw that at opposite sides of the lobby there were two ground-level doors, two spiral staircases leading upward, and two flights of steps going down, apparently to cellar dwellings. The ground-floor doors were numbered 15 and 16. The rest was guesswork. Gordon didn't like the look of the basements, and decided to try the upward steps next. He was lucky, and arrived first time at a doorway with '17' chalked on its paintless surface.

Standing at the closed door he felt once more the urge to run away, but he mastered it and knocked loudly. A wait of a minute or so, with heart thumping. No answer. Gordon knocked again. Still nobody came. He knocked a third time without result, then turned the knob and pushed the door. It was open.

There was no obvious reason why his knock hadn't been answered. The door opened straight into a living-room. A large, heavy woman sat on a sofa, looking at nothing in particular. She had a baby on her lap. A boy child, perhaps a year old, wearing nothing but a short vest, crawled on the bare board floor. Gordon closed the door quickly behind him so the child couldn't get out. A girl of two or three sat rocking in a very small rocking-chair. There was no other furniture.

The room was cold and fairly clean, its smell just a little sour. It didn't feel like anybody's home. The oddest thing about it was the silence. The mother turned her gaze on Gordon without much interest, saying nothing. Not a sound came from any of the three children, but the boy crawled to Gordon and began to drag himself upright, clutching his legs.

'I was looking for Sheila Woodrow,' Gordon said.

'She's in there,' said the woman, her voice unclear because she had no teeth. She pointed towards an inner door and was silent again.

Gordon put the boy back on the floor and crossed the room. Beyond it was a scullery, and bent down with her back to him, rubbing at the floor with a cloth, was Sheila. She hadn't heard him coming, and was talking to herself in a small clear voice:

'... and Cap'n Tony said, "Out of my way, villain," and the villain sprang towards him brandishing his sword, and steel clashed on steel, and Cap'n Tony drove the villain back until suddenly he dropped his sword and fled for dear life. Meanwhile, back at the camp under the palm trees, the beauteous Sheila had prepared a meal of yams and tropical fruits . . .'

'If it was me, I'd rather have fish and chips,' said Gordon.

Sheila sprang up and faced him. She was furious.

'Who said you could come here?' she demanded.

'I came to look for you.'

'Why? I didn't tell you to. Why couldn't you leave me alone?'

'You said I had to make a raft.'

'Did I?'

'Of course you did. Have you forgotten? It was to go to that pirate's island.'

'What pirate's island?'

'You know, the island in the canal. Where you said the pirate buried the treasure.'

'There never was any treasure,' said Sheila. 'Or any pirate either.' The anger went out of her and she started to cry, quietly. 'You shouldn't have come. I didn't want you to.'

'Well, you've been to my house.'

'Yes, and your mother sent me away. Of course she did.'

'I came to tell you I started making the raft. I'll have it ready in a day or two. And Mrs. Wallace told me to say she's got something for you.'

Sheila got down on her knees again and started dabbing at the floor.

'Do you *have* to do that?' Gordon asked.

'No, I don't. I don't have to do anything, nobody cares. I do it if I like.'

'Is that your mother?' Gordon could hardly believe that the large, vacant woman in the next room was related to thin, straight Sheila.

'No. My auntie. Well, my uncle's wife. My father died in the war, and they don't know where my mother is, and I came to live with my uncle.'

'Are they—are they kind to you?'

'Oh, they're all right. They don't take much notice of me at all. My auntie isn't very clever, but she manages, just about. Of course, Rod gets into a temper sometimes, but I keep out of his way.'

Gordon started.

'Rod?' he said. 'Rod Ridgeway?'

Sheila flushed.

'I can't help it,' she said. 'Yes, Rod and Tim live here as well. They're my sort-of cousins. You see, my auntie had them before she married my uncle. . . .'

'Golly!' said Gordon. 'It sounds complicated. How many more are there?'

'Oh, that's all. My uncle and auntie, and the three little ones you saw in the other room, and Rod and Tim, and me.'

'It's plenty, isn't it?'

'Yes, we're overcrowded,' she said in a matter-of-fact tone. 'Specially with Rod coming back from the Army. And he doesn't get on with my uncle. We could do with more rooms when they get arguing.'

An alarming thought occurred to Gordon.

'Is Rod around now?' he asked.

'Oh no. He's gone out. He won't be back till closing-time tonight.'

Sheila seemed to have calmed down a good deal by now. Gordon decided he could change back to his original subject.

'I've something else to tell you,' he said. 'I saw a chest in Nick Batten's window, just like a treasure-chest. With initials on it. "C.C." I expect they were burned on with a red-hot poker.'

Sheila dropped her floor-cloth into a bucket and wiped her face on her sleeve. She didn't say anything, but her eyes were interested.

'I thought it might have belonged to that pirate of yours,' Gordon said, 'only now it seems there never was one.'

She was recovering rapidly. A watery smile came to her face.

'You don't know,' she said. 'Perhaps there *was* one and he *did* bury a treasure.'

Gordon stared.

'I don't know where I am with you,' he complained. 'One minute you say one thing and the next minute you say the opposite.'

'Well, I was upset. But with "C.C." on the house and "C.C." on the chest, it must be true, mustn't it?'

'Seems to me,' said Gordon thoughtfully, 'that you don't even know whether to believe your own stories.'

Sheila looked down and said nothing.

'Anyway, listen. You've to go to Mrs. Wallace's, because she's got something for you. And on the way there you can have a look at that chest in Nick Batten's window. And then you can come and see the raft I'm making.'

'I can't come to your home, because your mum said I mustn't.'

'Tomorrow's Friday. My dad'll be out with the van all morning and my mum'll be in the shop. Come round to the back and tap at the window and it'll be all right.'

'Well, I don't know. I might.'

'You do. Come tomorrow. Think of Captain Cutlass.'

Gordon went out through the other room. Sheila came with him to the door. The mother, the little girl and the baby were all where they had been before, but the boy had fallen into the empty hearth and was whining quietly, unable to get out. Sheila picked him up automatically as she went past.

'If Rod's really after you, you'd better watch out, all the same,' she told Gordon as he left. 'He's still on his demob leave, and the pubs aren't open yet, so he might be anywhere.'

Gordon went down the stairs and out through the lobby as quickly as he could, casting nervous glances all around him. The stairway that led into the basement was particularly alarming— it was like a dark hole from which a goblin might spring. A rustling sound made him jump, but it was only the alley-cat, still prowling around the dustbin. He was glad to get into the street, and gladder still to get through the archway and back into the world outside the Shambles.

CHAPTER 7

On his way home, Gordon stopped to look again at the chest in Nick Batten's window. Unlike most of Mr. Batten's goods it was pleasant to look at—chunky and satisfying. He'd have liked to take it home with him. He wondered what "C.C." stood for. It couldn't really be Captain Cutlass. Sheila had made that name up. And the chest couldn't really be a treasure-chest—or at least, if it ever had been, the treasure must have been removed long before the chest finished up in the junkshop.

'Hullo, Porky,' said a well-known husky voice.

Gordon jumped. He'd looked out for Ridgeways and other enemies all the way back from the Shambles, but here, in the main shopping street of the Jungle, he'd felt safe and stopped bothering.

Now, just beside him, stood Tim Ridgeway, grinning. And behind Tim were his brother Rod, a bull-like figure in new ill-fitting civilian clothes, and a small, fair, wiry young man whom Gordon hadn't seen before.

'Hullo,' said Gordon. His heart thudded. He knew what they

wanted. But he moved casually away from the shop window and continued down Camellia Hill. After a few yards he glanced around. Rod and Tim and Rod's friend were following him, grinning. Gordon crossed the road to Hibiscus Street, carefully taking no notice. The three still followed.

Hibiscus Street was usually quite busy, and Gordon didn't think they'd attack him while people were around. With luck he might get safely to his father's shop at the bottom end. He walked on. The three behind had fallen into step with him and walked in menacing echo.

Half-way down the street they closed in. For the moment there was nobody near. Rod and the other young man seized an arm each and whisked Gordon into a side street, then into a narrow back entry.

'Didn't you want to talk to your old pals, Porky?' asked Tim, mockingly.

'Aw, stow it!' said Rod to Tim. He shoved a beefy unpleasant face down towards Gordon.

Rod was dangerous. Everyone knew Rod Ridgeway was dangerous. His temper was bad, his intelligence low, his physical strength enormous. One of these days he was going to hit somebody too hard. Then he'd be in trouble, and there were plenty who wouldn't be sorry—so long as they could avoid being the cause of it.

'You bin 'ittin' our Tim,' he said in a thick hoarse tone. 'Nobody 'its our flippin' kid and gets away with it.'

'Teach him a lesson, Rod,' said the small fair man.

'I don't need tellin' what to do, Walter Thompson,' said Rod. 'If our Tim needs bashin',' *I'll* bash 'im. But if anyone else tries it, I'll bash *them*.' He put a huge hand under Gordon's chin and jolted his head back. ' 'Oo do you think you are?' he demanded.

'Just a lump of fat from the porkshop,' said Walter wittily.

'You from Sid Dobbs's flippin' porkshop?' said Rod. 'Clever feller, that Sid Dobbs. Well, *you're* not so flippin' clever, Fatty. I'll show you.'

He'd taken his left hand from Gordon's chin. Now he drew back his right fist. Gordon was within a split second of being hit, hard. He tried an old trick.

'Look, there's the copper!' he cried.

Unexpectedly, it worked. Rod looked round. Walter slackened his grip on Gordon just long enough to let him jerk himself free. A moment later he was racing at top speed down Hibiscus Street.

The shop of S. Dobbs, pork butcher, was on the left-hand side near the bottom, at the corner of Mimosa Row. Gordon got there just ahead of Tim Ridgeway, flung the door open, slammed it behind him in Tim's face, and leaned on the marble counter inside, gasping for breath. Tim stayed outside. So did Walter when he arrived a moment afterwards. But Rod himself, last of the three to reach the shop, stumped straight in, and the other two followed him. Rod turned and kicked the door shut with a crash.

Gordon darted behind the counter. Mr. Dobbs's was usually a busy shop, but it happened to be empty except for the young girl, not long out of school, who worked as an assistant.

'Send us the gaffer!' ordered Rod.

The girl stared, wide-eyed and frightened. She knew Rod. Everyone in the Jungle knew Rod.

'Get a move on!' he said. 'The gaffer. The boss. Sid Dobbs. Tell 'im I want 'im!'

Sidney Dobbs appeared from the back.

'Well,' he said. 'What can I do for you?'

'This lad o' yours. 'E bashed our kid.'

'Oh, did he?' Mr. Dobbs looked from Gordon to Tim and back again. 'There's usually two sides to these matters. What did your brother do to *him*?'

Rod wasn't used to being answered back.

'Watch it!' he said threateningly. 'Watch it! I'm just tellin' you so that you'll know why your lad's gettin' a bashin' from me!'

'Get out of my shop!' said Mr. Dobbs. He was a small thin man but he wasn't a coward. He stepped smartly round the counter.

'Get out of—your—flippin'—shop?' repeated Rod. He stood, heavy and motionless. ''Oo are you to tell Rod Ridgeway what to do? Listen to me, Sid Dobbs. While you been makin' your pile out of the war, me an' Walter 'ere was fightin' for our country. Six year of it, that's what I've 'ad, and two of 'em in the glasshouse. An' I've no more in my pockets now than I 'ad at the start. An' then you tell me to get out of your shop? 'Ere's an answer for you, Sid Dobbs!'

Suddenly Rod acted. A shove sent Mr. Dobbs flying into the corner. A blow on the side of the head put Gordon down. A sweep of Rod's arm cleared the marble counter of its neat array of hams, sausages, brawns, potted meats. The weighing machine went over with a crash. Rod turned towards the window, wrenched out two wooden trays of pies and sausage-rolls, and sent those flying as well. It was all over in half a minute. Then, head down, he stumped out.

Walter and Tim looked at each other, half impressed, half scared, as if it was more than they'd expected.

'It was Rod what did all that,' said Walter. 'Nowt to do with me.' He helped Mr. Dobbs up from the floor. Then he and Tim followed Rod into the street. Tim closed the door behind him, carefully.

Gordon was dazed, but only for a moment. He picked himself up.

'Are you all right, Dad?' he asked.

Sidney Dobbs was clutching his stomach. Gordon fetched a chair from behind the shop. Mr. Dobbs sank into it. After a minute or so he grinned feebly.

'Winded, that's all, son.'

Then the grin faded.

'You didn't ought to have got that pair on to you. Rod Ridgeway and Walt Thompson, they're a bad lot. Brute force and low cunning, that's what they add up to. What were you doing?'

'Tim Ridgeway tried to bully me. I pushed him over.'

'Good for you.' Mr. Dobbs looked at his son with approval. 'You got to look after yourself in this world. Nobody else'll stick up for you. Don't let your mum make you soft. Anyway, let's hope those two are satisfied now.'

'The shop's in an awful mess, Dad,' said Gordon, looking round him.

'We'd better clear it up,' said Mr. Dobbs. 'Where's that Alice gone? Hopped it. Scared, I expect.'

Gordon and his father groped on the floor, picking up what had been knocked over, putting back shelves and trays, rejecting food that had got obviously dirty but wiping and replacing anything that didn't look too bad. They were interrupted two or three times by customers.

'Just a little accident,' was Mr. Dobbs's reply to inquiries. He sold a few pies at a discount as slightly damaged.

'Not as bad as it looks,' he said at length. 'Good job your mother wasn't here, though. I wish I knew where young Alice had got to. Floor could do with a good clean.'

It was just at that moment that Alice reappeared. She'd had more presence of mind than Mr. Dobbs thought, and had gone to fetch Police-Sergeant Hawkins. He was with her now—a grizzled man who'd have retired if it hadn't been for the war. He was tough, kindly, experienced, and long past being surprised by anything people did. He raised his eyebrows inquiringly towards Mr. Dobbs.

Gordon waited for the facts to come out. Alice listened eagerly, agog for sensation. But Mr. Dobbs didn't seem anxious to tell. "Morning, Sergeant,' he said. 'Not so nice for the time of year, is it?'

'You've had a spot of trouble, Mr. Dobbs, I believe.'

'A bit of an accident,' said Mr. Dobbs.

'An accident involving Rod Ridgeway and Walter Thompson?'

Mr. Dobbs nodded. There was a minute's silence. Then,

'Come on, Sid,' said Sergeant Hawkins. 'Let's be having it.'

Reluctantly Mr. Dobbs told the story. He made it appear that in a fit of annoyance Rod had gone farther than he intended.

'I don't want to get him into trouble,' he finished.

'I see,' said Sergeant Hawkins. 'People often don't want to get on the wrong side of Rod Ridgeway.' Mr. Dobbs said nothing.

'Time comes when these fellows have to be taught a lesson, all the same,' said the sergeant.

Mr. Dobbs still said nothing.

'But they're both just out of the Army,' said Sergeant Hawkins. 'Pity to have them in trouble so soon. I think I'll just give them a talking-to. Does that meet the situation, Mr. Dobbs?'

Mr. Dobbs nodded, relieved.

'That'd be fine,' he said. 'Don't tell them I complained, will you? In fact, I'd like you to tell them I *didn't* complain.'

Sergeant Hawkins sighed.

'I'll do just that,' he said. 'Good-bye, young Alice. You were quite right to come for me. Don't tell her off for that, Sid. 'Bye, Sid. 'Bye, sonny.' He went out.

'I'm glad to see the backs of the lot of them, police and all,' said Mr. Dobbs. 'Anything for a quiet life, that's my motto.'

Gordon was slightly shocked. 'You said you have to stick up for yourself,' he reminded his father.

'If you must, son,' said Mr. Dobbs. 'If you must, you must. But there's some folks that it's best not to get at loggerheads with. Anyway, let's hope we've seen the end of this matter. Look, here's old Mrs. Price coming in for her quarter pound of brawn. Not a word to her, or it'll be all round the neighbourhood.'

CHAPTER 8

Gordon banged a nail home with a last satisfying blow of his hammer, and turned to see Sheila watching him.

'So,' he said. 'You came.'

'Yes, I came. I didn't tap at your window after all, because I could hear the hammering and I knew what it would be. It's a lovely raft, Gordon.'

'I know it isn't quite like the pictures,' Gordon said. 'You don't see them hammering away for hours in the pictures and pulling nails out that have gone in wrong.'

'It's nicer than the pictures, that's what I think. And look, we'll be able to sit in that part that's made of the underneath of the table. We'll be ever so safe and comfortable. When shall we be ready to go to Pirate's Island?'

Gordon looked doubtful. Although the idea of sailing the raft was exciting, whenever he thought of actually taking it out on the black waters of the North-west Junction Canal he didn't feel too keen. His sense of caution was more strongly developed than his sense of adventure. It was the task of making the raft that he was finding unexpectedly enjoyable.

'You didn't really mean all that, did you?' he said. 'There isn't any treasure on that island, you know there isn't. Perhaps we could find somewhere a bit easier to try the raft. Like the brickyard pond, over in Claypits.'

'Of course I meant it,' said Sheila indignantly. 'Of course there's a treasure. What about Captain Cutlass's chest?'

'Captain Cutlass's chest isn't on the island,' Gordon said. 'It's in Nick Batten's junkshop.'

'I didn't see it there this morning,' Sheila said.

Gordon was surprised.

'Well, it was there yesterday,' he said. 'In the left-hand corner of the window, nearest Mr. Moult the newsagent's.'

'I'm sure it's not there now. It was a proper treasure-chest, you said?'

'It was a proper chest. I didn't say it was a treasure-chest. You can't have looked in the right place. Nick Batten doesn't sell things all that quickly. They stay in his window for months. Years, sometimes.'

'Well, come along and see for yourself, then.'

Gordon looked reluctant.

'I'd rather get on with the raft,' he said.

'You can get on with that any time. . . . You're not frightened, are you?'

Gordon put down the hammer.

'Did you know Rod and Tim Ridgeway and Walt Thompson set on to me yesterday?' he asked.

She took a step back.

'No, I didn't. I'm sorry, Gordon. I'm ever so sorry. But I can't help it. I can't do anything to stop them.'

'I know you can't,' said Gordon. And yet in some obscure way he felt she was partly to blame.

'So are you afraid they'll be after you again?' she asked.

'Not really. My dad thinks they'll have finished now. But my mum says I haven't to go out by myself.'

'Oh, well, if that's what your mum says. . . .'

'But my dad said she was daft.'

Sheila looked puzzled for a moment. Then she said,

'Which of them's boss?'

'That depends,' said Gordon. And then he grinned. 'All right, let's go.'

They walked warily up Hibiscus Street, keeping a lookout in

all directions, but there was no sign of enemies. They arrived at Nick Batten's shop in Camellia Hill. Gordon couldn't believe that the chest would really have gone from the window. But it had.

'Well, that's a surprise,' he said. 'Things don't usually come and go as fast as that. You see that old washstand in the corner? That's been there as long as I can remember.'

'Nobody would want that old washstand,' said Sheila. 'But I expect people would want a treasure-chest.'

'P'raps he's moved it,' said Gordon, 'and now it's somewhere else in the shop where we can't see it.'

'Well, go and ask him,' said Sheila.

Gordon didn't want to.

'Go on,' she said. 'You're not afraid.'

'You're always telling me I'm not afraid.'

'I'll come in with you if you like.'

They went into Mr. Batten's shop. It was dusty and cavernous, and the air was full of dry, ancient smells. The floorboards creaked under their feet. Nobody was about. Gordon and Sheila stood for some minutes, then walked round the shop, peering in all its cluttered corners, looking for the brassbound chest. But they didn't see it, and still nobody came.

On the counter stood a large handbell. They looked at it for some time, nudging each other.

'Go on,' said Sheila.

'Tell me I'm not afraid,' said Gordon.

'Of course you're not. So ring it.'

With sudden boldness Gordon seized the bell and rang it loudly. It made even more noise than they'd expected, echoing in the bare shop.

Still nobody came. Gordon rang the bell again and again, and then continuously, making an enormous din. Sheila, who rarely even smiled, began to giggle and then to laugh aloud. They were both of them silly and out of control as the bell rang and rang. And then Mr. Batten came in and said, 'Did you ring?', and they laughed and laughed again.

Nick Batten was a tall, thin, middle-aged man. He had a puzzled, strained expression, and one reason for this was that he was getting hard of hearing but didn't like to admit it. He had looked after an aged mother until the previous year. Now she was dead, and he didn't know what to do with himself. He had a small private income, which was just as well, because he wasn't much of a businessman and the shop barely paid its way.

'Well, what's the joke?' he asked.

'I'm sorry,' said Gordon. 'It just seemed funny. We rang and rang and rang, and then you said "Did you ring?"'

'Aye, well, maybe it seems funny to you,' said Mr. Batten, who'd only half heard the explanation but realized that it was something to do with his deafness. 'It's all right for you young 'uns. The day will come when you'll laugh the other sides of your faces. Oh aye, when I was a lad I thought life was funny. Little did I know. . . . Any road, what can I do for you?'

'We wondered what had happened to that chest you had in the window yesterday,' said Gordon.

'Speak up, lad, speak up.'

'The chest,' said Gordon more loudly. 'We wondered what had happened to it.'

'Oh, that,' said Mr. Batten. 'It's sold. A nice little job, that. They don't make 'em like that any more.'

Gordon and Sheila looked at each other.

'Ask him who bought it,' said Sheila.

As often before, Gordon found himself doing as she told him. He asked the question and repeated it twice before Mr. Batten understood. Luckily it didn't occur to him to say that it was none of the children's business.

'Old Arthur Kite bought it,' he said. 'Right taken with it, he was. Mind you, he got it cheap. I sold him it for two pound. I was thinking I'd paid thirty shilling for it, so I'd have made ten bob profit. And then I remembered afterwards, it was fifty shilling I paid, not thirty. Eh dear, since my mam passed away I sometimes don't know what I'm doing.'

'Who's Arthur Kite?' asked Gordon.

'You know Arthur Kite. He lives down by the viaduct on the canal bank. Gumble's Yard, they call it. There's a row of cottages, and then there's this place above them where Arthur lives. Go up the iron staircase at the end.'

Sheila now stood on tiptoe to ask Mr. Batten a question.

'Where did it come *from,* Mr. Batten?' she asked.

'Eh,' said Mr. Batten in a tone of mild puzzlement. 'You do ask some questions. I don't know why you're so curious about that chest, I really don't.' But it still didn't occur to him to tell the children to mind their own business.

'It came from the Vicarage,' he said. 'Mrs. Wallace, the Reverend's wife, brought it in the other day. Said it had been in the attic for donkeys' years, and then something that somebody said had put her in mind of it. She thought it might be valuable. "Mrs. Wallace,' I said, "if we was in South Kensington, London"—that's a right posh place, you know—"if we was in South Kensington, London, I dare say we'd get every penny of a fiver for it, but here in the Jungle it's just an old box to put things in. Thirty bob." And she looked at me as if I was diddling her, so I gave her fifty bob instead. And then I forgot and sold it for two pound to old Arthur. So it wasn't much of a bargain for me. And now you know all about it. Why don't you go an' play? Come back on Guy Fawkes' Night and I might give you something for your bonfire.'

Mr. Batten was still laughing heartily at this joke about the value of his stock when the children went out.

CHAPTER 9

'Well,' said Gordon. 'Fancy it coming from Mrs. Wallace!'

'I don't think that's surprising,' said Sheila. 'The Vicarage was "C.C.'s" house, and this is "C.C.'s" chest. Where else should it come from but the Vicarage?'

'But fancy it happening just now. After all these years.'

'You heard what Mr. Batten said. He said something had put Mrs. Wallace in mind of it. I expect the something that put her in mind of it was us, asking questions.'

'It still seems funny to me,' said Gordon. 'I told her I'd seen the chest in the shop, and she as good as told me to mind my own business. And that reminds me. Did you call, like she said, for whatever it was she wanted to give you?'

'Yes, I called on my way down to your house.'

'It must have been a little parcel this time,' said Gordon. 'Not like the big one she gave you the other day.'

Sheila looked uneasy.

'Yes, it was,' she said. 'A very little one.' But she didn't offer to tell him anything more.

Gordon wasn't inquisitive by nature, and he let that subject drop. But he was still puzzled about the chest.

'She must have known it was there,' he said. 'And perhaps there are other things in the attic as well that belonged to "C.C." But I wouldn't like to ask her. She'd tell me to mind my own business again.'

'I expect she would,' said Sheila. For a moment she looked downcast. Then she brightened.

'We could get Tony Boyd to ask her,' she said. 'He often goes to the Vicarage. He knows them well. If she told anybody, she'd tell *him*.'

Gordon had been afraid he was going to find himself on the Vicarage doorstep once more, with Sheila nudging him to put questions to an irritated Mrs. Wallace. He was glad of any suggestion that would let him out of that.

'Yes, we'll get Tony to do it,' he said with relief.

He looked up at the clock that was over the bank in Camellia Hill.

'Quarter to eleven,' he said. 'My mum'll come in to make my dinner at twelve. And seeing I'm not supposed to be out, I'd better be back by then.'

'All right,' said Sheila. 'We'll just have time to go down to Gumble's Yard.'

'Why should we go to Gumble's Yard?'

'To see that old man, of course, who bought the chest. Old Mr. Kite.'

'I don't see the point of that,' said Gordon. 'There won't be anything in the chest now. I'd have thought the only way to find anything out about it would have been to trace it back.'

'I want to look at the chest myself,' said Sheila. 'I haven't seen it yet. Come on, Gordon.'

Gordon opened his mouth to argue, but before he could say anything he found himself walking down Hibiscus Street with her.

'And so the old man sat by the fire-side,' she said dreamily, half to herself, 'feasting his eyes on the beautiful brass-bound treasure-chest that glowed so mellowly. Little did he know of Captain Cutlass, the menace of the Spanish Main, or of his grandson, the black-bearded stranger with the wooden leg. . . .'

'Oh, so old Black-bearded-Pegleg's back in the story, is he?' said Gordon.

Sheila looked at him reproachfully and said no more.

At the bottom of Hibiscus Street, they turned left along Canal Street. This was a dead end, cut off by the railway viaduct. The area between Canal Street and the canal itself had once been Gumble's Wharf, but bombs had dropped on it during the war and now there was nothing left but a row of decrepit cottages and a few outbuildings.

Gordon and Sheila walked past the front of the cottages and round to the gable end of the row. It faced on to the supports of the viaduct, only a few feet distant. High up in it was a door, approached from outside by an iron staircase rather like a fire-escape.

'That's where old man Kite lives,' Gordon said. He'd remembered Arthur Kite quite well when Mr. Batten jogged his memory. Some said the old man was a bit queer in the head, but he always seemed harmless. You saw him pushing an ancient pram around the Jungle, shopping for tiny quantities of this and that, bargaining for leftovers, or perhaps poking around on bombed sites, where he would make mysterious finds and tuck them furtively out of sight. He was generally supposed to be very poor.

'Go on,' said Sheila, nudging Gordon as usual. And for once Gordon felt brave. He seemed to be leading a risky, adventurous life these days. He set off boldly up the staircase, his boots clashing on the metal treads, and knocked loudly at Arthur Kite's door.

The door was opened at once, but only by an inch or two. A blue eye, under a white eyebrow, peered out.

'What do *you* want?' asked a high reedy voice.

'You bought a chest from Nick Batten's shop,' said Gordon.

'What if I did?'

'My friend would like to see it. If you don't mind, that is. She's interested in pirates—I mean she's interested in chests.'

'What friend? I can't see any friend.' The high voice was sharp and impatient.

'Down below,' said Gordon.

Mr. Kite opened the door a little wider and peered round. Sheila had a foot on the bottom step of the iron staircase.

'Is there just her?' he asked.

'Yes.'

'Sure it's only her? Nobody waiting round the corner?'

'There's nobody else,' Gordon assured him.

'All right. She can come up. Quickly, now.'

Sheila ran up the steps. Mr. Kite bundled the two of them through the door. Then he stepped outside, looked quickly round, came in, closed the door and shot the bolt.

'Can't be too careful,' he said. 'I don't trust people these days. Knock you down as soon as look at you, some of them would.'

Gordon and Sheila blinked in the half-light of Mr. Kite's dwelling. It was a long low attic that ran right along the top of the row of cottages underneath. The walls sloped so that a tall person could only have stood upright along the centre ridge. There were three small windows, but they didn't let much light in. In the middle was a closed stove, with a pipe going up to the roof. There was a camp-bed with Army blankets, a deal table, a chair, an old pricked rug on the floor. The general effect was clean but threadbare.

That was the effect of Mr. Kite, too. He was small and thin, with wispy white hair, and he wore a neat but patched suit and a collar and tie. He'd obviously shaved that day, and had cut himself two or three times. The children couldn't have guessed his age, but in the Jungle it was reckoned by the few who were interested that old man Kite was on the wrong side of eighty.

'Well?' he said sharply. 'Well?'

'We just wondered if we could have a look at the chest, that's all.'

'Who sent you? Did someone send you? Was it the bank, wanting to know where I've put my money?'

'Nobody sent us.'

'Why do you want to see the chest, then? What's your reason? There must be a reason.'

'It was just the initials on it that interested us,' said Gordon, 'because they're the same as the ones over the Vicarage door.'

'You've seen it already!' said Mr. Kite at once. 'You must have done. Or you wouldn't have known about the initials. Why do you want to see it again?'

'I only saw it in Mr. Batten's window,' said Gordon. 'I didn't get much of a look.'

'I haven't seen it at all,' said Sheila.

Mr. Kite thought for a moment.

'You can see the outside,' he said. 'I'm not showing you what's in it. Oh, no. I'm not stupid, you know. I'm not stupid.'

He motioned to the children to sit down on the camp-bed.

'Now, look the other way. Towards the door. Don't turn round till I tell you.'

Obediently Gordon and Sheila sat with their eyes on the outer door. There were scrabbling sounds in a corner behind them.

'Are you watching?' demanded the sharp reedy voice.

'No.'

'All right. Just a moment now. There, you can look.'

On the table in front of them, between Mr. Kite's hands, was the dome-lidded, brass-bound chest. It was more beautiful than when Gordon had seen it in the junkshop window. Mr. Kite had polished it until it glowed. And a frail glow of pride lit up the old man himself. For all his caution, he'd obviously been longing to show it to somebody.

'Isn't it lovely?' he asked. 'Eh? Isn't it lovely?'

'Oh, it is!' said Sheila. It was something new in her life. Most things in the Jungle were cheap, ill-made, to be used and discarded. The chest was a piece of fine craftsmanship, smooth, precise, built to last. And it had lasted, and with luck it would last for many years after everyone now seeing it was dead.

'I know what you're thinking,' said Mr. Kite. 'You think an old man of my age shouldn't be so extravagant. That's what you think. Oh, I know. I can tell. Two pounds I paid for that. I can live for a month on two pounds. The old man's a fool, you say to yourselves.'

'We don't,' said Gordon.

'Oh, no, we don't!' said Sheila, still entranced. The beauty of the chest was increased for her by the aura that hung about it —the aura of adventure in far places. She thought of green islands in the blue Pacific, or perhaps the blue Caribbean, she didn't mind which. She thought of palm-trees and tall ships. And, of course, of pirates and treasure. A fair wind filled the sails of her fancy. Gumble's Yard, Canal Street, the whole grey dirty city of Cobchester, sank quietly below the horizon.

'Well, I'm not such a fool as you think,' said Mr. Kite. 'I've got a use for this chest. I didn't buy it just to look at. Oh, no. I may be old but I'm still all there, you know.' He tapped his forehead. 'Too smart for some of them, I can tell you. Banks! You know something about banks?'

Sheila, thousands of miles away, heard not a word. Gordon tried hard to look interested.

'They're not safe!' said Mr. Kite. 'Young Walter Thompson told me so last week. And he should know, he has a pal who works in one. Banks have been living on borrowed money for years, he says. Might crash any time, he says. "If I was you," he says, "I'd take it all out while you can." '

The old man was gleefully excited.

'So I did! I drew out every penny! If the banks go down now, they won't take *my* savings down with them. I'm keeping the money where I can watch over it myself.'

He patted the chest.

'It's a pal to me already!' he said. And then he was wary once more. 'Now, both of you look the other way again. It's nothing to do with you!'

There were more scrabblings in the corner before Mr. Kite told the children they could look round. And having put the chest away he seemed quickly to lose interest.

'You've seen it now,' he said. 'That should satisfy you. Don't start telling people. I mind my own business and other folks can mind theirs. And watch your step, now, as you go down those stairs.'

'Well,' said Gordon when he and Sheila were back in Canal Street. 'It looks as if the chest's a treasure-chest again. Mr. Kite's keeping his savings in it.'

Sheila wasn't much interested in Mr. Kite's savings.

'It's the loveliest thing I ever saw, Gordon. And just seeing it is like being in a story. I want to know how it got from Captain Cutlass to the antique shop. And what happened to *his* treasure.'

'If any,' said Gordon. He was thoughtful. 'Mr. Kite mentioned Walter Thompson,' he said. 'That's Rod Ridgeway's pal.'

Sheila was away again, not listening.

'It'd be hard luck on Mr. Kite,' said Gordon after a minute or two, 'if anybody came treasure-hunting down here in Gumble's Yard.'

There still wasn't any response.

'Seems to me,' Gordon added, 'that we've got another reason for seeing Tony Boyd.'

This brought her back to earth.

'Oh, yes!' she said, eyes shining. 'Let's go and see Tony. Let's go and see him this afternoon!'

CHAPTER 10

Tony Boyd was often at the Vicarage, and sometimes stayed
for a few days at a time. Mr. and Mrs. Wallace had given him
a room of his own, which he was expected to keep clean. The
Vicarage had fourteen rooms, half of which were spare, and
Mrs. Wallace wasn't sorry to have one of them occupied and
looked after.

When the children arrived, the Vicar sent them straight up.
Tony's room, on the second floor, had a bed and a table and
a cupboard and a great many books, and there wasn't room
for much else. Tony was making toast at the gas-fire. He
toasted extra slices for the children. Gordon was hungry, because it was an hour and a half since he'd had his dinner. He
ate heartily. Sheila just nibbled. No wonder she was thin, he
thought.

'Well,' said Tony, when they'd told him about the chest's
appearance in Mr. Batten's window, 'it does sound odd. I'll
find a way of asking Mrs. Wallace if I can. But it's easy to put

a foot wrong with her.'

'I bet it is!' said Gordon.

At Sheila's suggestion, and to Gordon's relief, they'd only told Tony about the similarity of initials. They'd said nothing about maps or islands or mysterious strangers with wooden legs. Gordon didn't think Tony would be impressed by such tales. He smiled when Tony said jokingly,

'Who knows, it might be a pirate's treasure-chest.'

'Oh, it is!' Sheila assured him. She seemed pleased that he'd understood so soon. 'That's just what it is, a pirate's treasure-chest!'

Tony raised his eyebrows.

'She's like that all the time,' said Gordon tolerantly. 'She wouldn't be surprised if a pirate came round the corner any minute.'

'Well, Sheila's got one under her own roof just now,' said Tony. 'Or at any rate, somebody who *looks* like one. Have you seen Rod Ridgeway today, Gordon?'

'No,' said Gordon. 'And I don't want to, thank you.'

'It seems Rod had an argument with somebody in the *George* the other night,' said Tony. 'He got a cut eye. He'll be wearing a patch on it for about a fortnight. Apparently it's nothing much—nothing at all compared with what the other fellow got. But this is what makes it so funny, Gordon. He's wearing a *black* patch!'

'Oh, that was my idea,' said Sheila calmly.

'*Your* idea?'

'Yes. He was wearing a pink patch yesterday. I told him it ought to be black. He said, "Get out of the way and mind your own business." But he must have thought it was a good suggestion.'

'You'd better be careful what ideas you put into people's heads, Sheila!' said Tony, smiling. 'Because they certainly seem to catch on. You have quite a gift for making people do things.'

'She has that!' said Gordon with feeling.

'I must say, Rod looks a fearful sight,' Tony said. 'And well he knows it. As if he didn't frighten people enough already. This would make anybody run a mile!'

'Talking of Rod,' said Gordon, 'do you know anything about his pal, Walter Thompson?'

'The little thin fellow?' said Tony. 'Not much. He lives with his married brother Clifford in Orchid Grove. Cliff and Betty

Thompson are very decent people. But as for Walter, well, he's a bit of an artful dodger. I think he's been in trouble now and then. Nothing serious, but he's a worry to them.'

'He told Mr. Kite to take his money out of the bank and keep it in a box,' said Gordon.

'How silly,' said Tony. And then, after a moment, as a thought seemed to strike him,

'Oh, did he? And what did Mr. Kite do?'

'He bought the chest. The chest we were telling you about, that came from Mrs. Wallace. And his money must be in it now. Down in Gumble's Yard.'

'I don't like that,' said Tony. He considered it for a moment. I'll ask the Vicar to have a word with Mr. Kite and persuade him that the British banks aren't really going to crash by this time tomorrow. The old chap ought certainly to keep his money somewhere safer. And in the meantime—look, why don't we go down to Orchid Grove and talk to the Thompsons? If Walter's got some silly scheme in his head, maybe they'll put him off it.'

'I can't come now,' said Sheila. 'I've got to do something.'

Gordon looked at her curiously.

'It's—it's to do with that present Mrs. Wallace gave me,' said Sheila. Gordon realized that this was a subject it wasn't tactful to ask questions about. He let it pass. Tony turned out the gas-fire and they trooped downstairs and out of the Vicarage front door. Sheila went off towards the Wigan Road. Tony and Gordon walked down Hibiscus Street to Orchid Grove. It was a narrow terrace of squat, grimy houses, typical of the Jungle, though Number 40 was set apart from its neighbours by spotless paintwork and a doorstep scoured to creamy cleanness.

'I bet it isn't Walter who keeps it like that,' said Tony as he knocked.

The door opened instantly.

'Did I hear my name taken in vain?' asked Walter. He'd obviously just been going out. 'Hullo, it's the Band of Hope. The Vicar's Assistant, any road. Master Boyd in person. Been having a nice holy time, young Tony?'

'Tell them to come in, Walt,' said a voice from somewhere behind.

'Aye, well, I'd rather see even you than that flipping copper,' said Walter. 'Reading me the Riot Act about how to behave myself in pork-shops. I told him it wasn't me that did the damage, but that didn't shut him up. Truth is, there's no holding

Rod when he gets one of his moods on him. . . . Hey!' He looked at Gordon with slight alarm. 'You're Sid Dobbs's lad, aren't
you? What you want here? Your dad's not getting any money
out of me. It was Rod what did it.'

'It wasn't about that, Mr. Thompson,' said Tony. 'We came
to see your brother and his wife.'

'Aye, well, there's no charge for that,' said Walter. 'Help
yourselves.' He called over his shoulder,

'Hey, Cliff, there's company for you. Tony Boyd and friend.
And ta-ta for now, I'm off to meet Rod.'

'Just a minute, Walt.' Clifford Thompson joined them in the
doorway. 'You know what Sergeant Hawkins said. He said if
you've any sense you'll keep away from Rod. And he meant
from now on, not from next week. Rod'll land you in court
before long if you stick with him.'

'Aw, stow it, Cliff!' said Walter. 'It's bad enough getting all
that from old Hawkins, without getting it from you as well.
You think I'm the poor little brother, easily led, don't you?
Well, you can think again. Rod and me's partners. I've got
more ideas than him, I can tell you. Rod's got brawn all right,
but I've got summat scarcer. And you know what that is?'
He pointed significantly to his head.

'Brains!' he said.

'I wish you'd enough of them to steer clear . . .' Clifford began. But Walter wasn't going to listen. He made a rude noise,
and had gone and closed the door before Clifford could finish
the sentence.

Clifford took Tony and Gordon into the living-kitchen, where
Betty Thompson was ironing in front of the fire. She was in her
middle twenties—thin, pale, worried-looking, with straight mou-
sy hair and slightly prominent grey eyes. Clifford was not unlike Walter, but a shade taller and more solidly built.

'Eh, I wish we knew what to do with your Walt,' said Betty
to Clifford. 'He seems worse since he came out of the Army.'

'I keep saying, it's that Rod Ridgeway.'

'I know, love. But it's no good going on at him. The more
you try to put him off, the less notice he takes.' Betty stood
her iron on its end. 'Hullo, Tony. How about a cup of tea?
Kettle's on the hob.'

Tony accepted the offer. Betty brewed tea and poured out
for them all.

'You look tired,' Tony said.

'I am tired. Little Jenny's not well again. She seems to be always ailing.' Betty sighed. 'It's not good for her here. Damp, you know.'

'Why don't you leave?' asked Gordon.

'Where d'you think we'd go?' said Clifford. 'You don't get houses just by asking for them. We've been on the list long enough. But you can stay on it till you die of old age for all the chance you've got.'

For a moment he sounded bitter.

'The Vicar tried to get us priority,' he said, 'with Jenny not being well. But it seems there are plenty worse off than us. And Orchid Grove isn't even condemned.'

'Cheer up, love,' said Betty. 'At least we've got a roof over our heads. We'll have to dream the rest. Like I do sometimes. A cottage in the country, and Jenny well again, and maybe two more children—I think that would be enough. . . .'

'It would that!' said Clifford.

'A boy and another girl, that's what I'd like. I know what I want to call the next two. Kevin and Sandra. I wonder if we'll ever have them.'

'We might have them, but we'll never have the country cottage,' said Clifford. 'No work in the country in my trade. And Betty, love, there's no point in dreaming. You'll be like little Sheila if you go on that way.'

'Oh aye, Sheila,' said Betty. 'Poor child, there's nothing for *her* but dreams . . . Tony, have another cup of tea. And there's some biscuits in that tin.'

'Tony hasn't told us yet what he's come for,' said Clifford.

'It's about Walter, I'm afraid,' said Tony.

'What's he been up to now?'

'Well, nothing yet. But he persuaded old Mr. Kite to draw his money out of the bank and keep it in a box in his home. He said the banks weren't safe.'

'Oh, Walter always thinks he knows best,' said Clifford.

'Yes, but what if there was another reason?' said Tony.

'I don't follow you . . . Oh, I see. You mean . . . you can't mean he might be planning to pinch the money?'

'Well, I don't know,' said Tony. 'Perhaps I'm being unfair to him.'

'And perhaps you're not,' said Clifford. 'I wouldn't put it past him. Still, it would be a bit obvious, wouldn't it? Walter tells the old chap to take his money out of the bank, and soon afterwards it disappears. Who's going to be suspected? No prize for guessing the answer. Walter. '

'Would Walt think as far ahead as that?' asked Betty. 'You know what he is. It'd be just like him to cook up a daft scheme, and fancy himself as a right Clever Dick, without stopping to consider what'd happen afterwards.'

'Well, there's no telling with Walt,' admitted Clifford. 'Thank you for warning us, Tony. We'll have a word with him later on. Drop a strong hint, like. But mind you, Walt's apt to go his own way, whatever anyone says.'

'Just think, Cliff,' said Betty. 'Apart from your brother Bob, over in Yorkshire, Walt's the only living relative we've got. We'd better watch out crossing the road, love. If anything happened to us, Walt might be left in charge of little Jenny.'

'Not to mention Kevin and Sandra,' said Clifford.

Betty smiled, an unexpectedly lovely smile. Then she sat up suddenly.

'Listen to that cough,' she said. 'That's Jenny again. Eh, we've enough to worry about with the one we've got, never mind the ones we might have some day. I wish we could get that room dry. Give them some more tea, Cliff, while I go up to her.'

CHAPTER 11

'There, it's finished,' said Gordon.

Sheila looked with admiration at the upturned table, roughly nailed to a row of planks. Beside it were two paddles, made from left-over bits of floorboard fastened to broom handles.

'It's lovely, Gordon,' she said. 'You *are* clever.'

'Oh, it's just an ordinary raft,' he said. But he felt pleased with himself, all the same. He, Gordon, had made it. He could make things. He would make cupboards, bookshelves, elaborate surprises for his parents. They would be astonished by his craftsmanship. . . .

'What shall we call it—I mean her?' Sheila asked.

Gordon hadn't thought until that moment of naming his raft. He looked blank.

'We'll call her *Hispaniola*!' said Sheila. 'Like in *Treasure Island*.'

It seemed a bit fancy to Gordon. But he didn't feel like arguing—especially as he thought she'd probably get her way in the end.

'All right,' he said.

'And when are we sailing to *our* Treasure Island?' she went on.

'Listen,' said Gordon patiently. 'If that chest really was a treasure-chest . . .'

'It is!' she declared with conviction. 'It is!'

'Well, then, use your brains. It's not buried on the island, is it?'

'No,' said Sheila, in a reasonable tone. 'No, I suppose it's not.' But the logic of a situation never seemed to have much effect on her. Here was the raft, and out there in the canal was the island, and she wanted to go to it.

'We could look for the place where the chest might have been buried long ago,' she said. 'There might even still be something in the hole, if they hadn't been very careful getting it out. Some pieces-of-eight left over, like there were in a story I read.'

'You and your stories,' said Gordon. But now that it was finished he had more confidence than before in his raft's seaworthiness. He was as eager now to try it out as she was.

'We can't go to the island in broad daylight,' he said. 'It's too near to all the wharves. There are still Canal Company people about in the daytime, tidying things up. They'd be sure to see us. But we could go after tea some day, when they've gone home and it's getting dark.'

Sheila's face fell.

'I wanted to try it *now*,' she said in a small voice.

'Well, p'r'aps we could just have a very short sail now, and see how we get on. We can go from Gumble's Yard, this side of the viaduct. There won't be anyone there to stop us.'

Sheila brightened at once.

'The launching of the *Hispaniola*!' she said. 'Her maiden voyage. Yes, of course, it would spoil it if we did everything at once. We'll sail for treasure another day, after we've taken stores aboard and looked out for stowaways.'

'There's not much room for stowaways,' said Gordon.

'No, well, perhaps not. Still, we can't have everything, can we? But Gordon, how will we get her down to Gumble's Yard?'

Gordon had thought of this already. Among the contents of the outhouse was his own old perambulator. His parents had put it by, like so many other things, in case it was needed again. But it never had been. He dragged it out, oiled its squeaking axles and wrenched off the tattered remnants of the hood. With much effort they raised the raft between them and balanced it across the rusty carcase of the pram.

'We'll need a rope,' said Gordon. A reckless spirit was getting into him. He stripped two or three nondescript items from his mother's clothes-line and left them hanging over the edge of the water-butt. And in a moment the line itself was lying coiled on the deck of the *Hispaniola*.

They opened the back-yard gate and pushed the raft out into Mimosa Row. It was awkward to manoeuvre, being much too wide for its wheelbase. But the way was downhill, and they managed without too much difficulty to get it as far as Canal Street. They pushed it past the row of cottages, round the gable end where the staircase led to Mr. Kite's attic, and on to the old Gumble's Wharf, now disused. There was a drop of about two feet to the black, unwholesome-looking water.

Gordon fastened one end of his mother's clothes-line to the raft, and the other to one of the great iron rings that remained from the days when the wharf had been in use. Then they pushed the pram as near as they dared to the edge of the quay, and tipped the raft over. There was a moment when it looked as if it would finish in the water upside-down. But it righted itself and floated, with only a slight list to one side. Gordon and Sheila looked at it with pride and pleasure. The upturned table formed a shallow well in which there was room for both of them.

'Well, go on, get in,' said Sheila.

Gordon felt a return of his old nervousness. He wasn't used to this kind of activity. But he took a deep breath and jumped from the wharf into the well of the raft. He had a moment's panic as it rocked under his weight and water washed over its planks at the lower side. But soon it steadied itself. Sheila handed him the paddles, then sat on the edge of the wharf and held out her hands trustingly for him to jump her down. She was so light that this time the raft hardly stirred. They sat side by side, wedged comfortably between the kitchen-table's upturned legs, giggling at each other. Above them a steam-train chugged over the viaduct and something fell on to the water a few feet away from them. It was a half-eaten sandwich. They giggled again.

Gordon realized that they were still moored. He stood up to free the rope from the iron ring, and the raft tilted alarmingly as he leaned over. He had another moment's panic as the gap between raft and wharf widened while he was still fumbling, but his slip-knot gave way just in time and he sat safely down beside Sheila. *Hispaniola* was afloat on her own.

The raft was heavy, and hard to steer. But they were elated—Gordon at the success of his carpentry, Sheila at the romance of being on the water. The next half-hour was sheer enjoyment. They managed to propel themselves a hundred yards or so along the canal, passing under the viaduct. But they turned back before rounding the bend that would have brought them into view from the Canal Company's premises.

As they came back towards Gumble's Yard, it occurred to Gordon that he might have difficulty in geting ashore. It had been easy enough to jump down to the raft, but it wouldn't be so easy to scramble up from it. He muttered something to Sheila about his doubts, but she only looked trustingly at him and said,

'Of *course* you'll manage.'

Luckily, just as they approached the wharf, old Mr. Kite appeared with his shopping-basket from the direction of Hibiscus Street. He didn't seem surprised to see them. He put his basket down on the iron staircase that led to his home, then came to the water's edge.

'Having a bit of fun, eh?' he said. 'Takes me back to when I was a lad. Always adventurous, I was. But you want to watch out. If you were drowned, you'd be sorry.'

He helped the children up from the raft, and the three of them manhandled it ashore.

'Don't bother taking it away with you,' he said. 'Put it in my shed.'

Among the tumbledown outbuildings of Gumble's Yard was a creosoted shed with 'A. Kite' over the door. There was a rusty padlock, but it seemed to be more for show than security, and Mr. Kite opened it without a key. Inside was a pile of lumber. The raft went in quite easily on top of the heap.

'I hope it'll be safe,' Gordon said.

'Of course it'll be safe,' said the old man. 'Nobody goes in Arthur Kite's shed. "Nothing worth stealing there," they say to themselves. And they're right. And anyway, who'd want your raft when there's a proper boat in the big shed ten yards away? Belongs to the Canal Company, that does, and it's time they put it somewhere safer. The lock's no better than mine. I wouldn't be a bit surprised if some young chaps was to break in and take *that* out for a jaunt. But your raft —no, you don't have to worry. It's as safe in there as my money is in the chest.'

'That's a lovely chest,' said Sheila, wistfully.

'You don't need to tell me. I get fonder of it every day. I look at it and I say to myself, "You're not such a fool as they think, Arthur Kite. You know a good bit of workmanship when you see it. You got your money's worth for that two pounds." That's what I say to myself.'

Mr. Kite put the rusty padlock back on the hasp.

'Get your raft out any time you like,' he told the children. 'Just twist the lock and it'll open.' And then he returned happily to the subject of his money and the chest and the insecurity of banks.

'That bank in Camellia Hill's still open,' he said. 'People going in and out as usual. But it'll crash soon, and that's a fact. I felt sorry for all those folks that rely on it. But they won't listen to an old man, you know. They won't listen to an old man. The Vicar himself came to see me last night. Told me my money wasn't safe. "It's never been safer in my life," I said. "I can keep an eye on it here. When it's in the bank I don't know what they're doing with it." But I couldn't persuade him, and he couldn't persuade me.'

Gordon and Sheila thanked Mr. Kite and set off towards Mr. Dobbs's shop, pushing the pram that had formerly carried their raft.

'Well, we're all ready to sail now,' said Sheila happily. 'Except that we ought to have some provisions for the voyage.'

'It's not going to take us *months* to get to the island,' said Gordon. 'About twenty minutes, I should think.'

Still, the thought of provisions was an attractive one. He knew Sheila couldn't bring anything. But when you lived at a pork-butcher's shop, supplies of food were no problem, even while rationing was still on. He could get something together quite easily. They could have a picnic on the raft, and maybe another on the island. It was an excellent idea.

'All right,' he said. 'Leave that to me.'

'And I'll bring Shippy the ship's cat,' said Sheila.

This puzzled Gordon at first. But then he remembered something she'd said the first time she went to his house.

'Not the white Persian ship's cat you were telling my mum about?' he said.

'Yes. Well, he's not as white as he used to be, but he's still my ship's cat.'

Gordon didn't believe for a moment that Shippy the ship's cat existed, but he'd learned that there was no point in arguing with Sheila on such matters.

'Just as you like,' he said. 'I'll meet you at Gumble's Yard after tea tomorrow. Six o'clock. Is that all right?'

'Aye, aye, Cap'n,' said Sheila.

Gordon liked the sound of that. He felt like a captain. He was in command of his own vessel, the *Hispaniola*. He was setting out tomorrow on an important voyage.

He stuck out his chest, and pushed the rusty pram with a swagger towards Mr. Dobbs's back-yard.

CHAPTER 12

Next day Gordon took a couple of pork pies, four sausage-rolls and a piece of polony from the shop, and put them in a biscuit-tin. And after tea he set off for Gumble's Yard. It was a chilly evening, and he was a few minutes ahead of time. Partly to keep warm, he dragged the raft out of Mr. Kite's shed and down to the edge of the water, but decided to wait until Sheila came before launching it.

She wasn't there at six, or a quarter past, or half past. The light began to fail. Gordon felt hungry, and ate one of the pies and two of the sausage-rolls. At a quarter to seven she still hadn't come, and it was clearly too late to start the voyage that evening. Cold and irritated, Gordon ate the other pie and the other two sausage-rolls. At seven o'clock he ate the polony as well. Then he dragged the raft back to Mr. Kite's shed, tucked the biscuit-tin under his arm, and stumped crossly home.

He thought Sheila would probably arrive with an explanation during the next day, but she didn't. After tea he went down to Gumble's Yard with fresh provisions, thinking she might have failed to get away and might turn up a day late. It was chilly again, and he stood for some time on the wharf, stamping his feet and trying to keep warm. There was still no Sheila. He ate the food and went home.

Next morning he wondered whether to go round to the Shambles and look for her. But he was a bit frightened of the Shambles, and especially of Number 17 since he'd learned that Rod lived there. And he hadn't enjoyed his visit to Sheila's home. There was something about it that chilled his spirits.

Besides, he felt aggrieved. The whole expedition had been her idea, and he'd taken a lot of trouble over it, and now she'd let him down. He wasn't going to bother any more. The *Hispaniola's* first trip could be its last for all he cared.

Still, he'd quite liked making the raft, and he wouldn't mind trying his hand at some other kind of woodwork. His mother had been urging her husband for months to put up a shelf in the kitchen. Gordon decided to surprise her by doing it himself while she was out. He had a fairly sound plank left over from the raft, and he spent one-and-sixpence of his own money on a pair of brackets. But the result, he had to admit, was crooked and rickety, and he knocked down quite a bit of plaster.

Mrs. Dobbs was houseproud and not very imaginative, and the one sin she couldn't forgive, even in Gordon, was making a mess. She didn't even pretend to look pleased. She told him off roundly. He tried not to be discouraged, and asked his father to buy the materials to make a cupboard or a bookcase. But Mr. Dobbs had business problems on his mind and couldn't be bothered.

Gordon relapsed into reading comics, listening to the radio and helping himself at intervals from the shop. Mrs. Dobbs was always glad to see him nibbling. She felt he needed to keep his strength up.

'I'm pleased you're staying at home, dear,' she told him. 'East, West, home's best, that's what they say.' But he began to get bored and sulky. Friday morning came, and the endless dreariness of the weekend loomed ahead. Suddenly Gordon knew that his fear and distaste must be overcome. He must go and find out what had happened to Sheila.

He made his way without incident up Hisbiscus Street, eastward along the Wigan Road, and down Slaughter Street towards the archway that led into the Shambles. He didn't dare to stop down, in case his courage failed him. He marched through the arch, along the narrow alley to the left, in at the third entry, and up the stairs that led from the dark lobby. He rapped smartly at the door that had '17' chalked on it, and when nobody came he rapped a second time, then pushed it open.

The room where the woman had sat with the baby and the two small children was empty. Gordon walked through it and looked in at the kitchen. That was empty, too. Beyond it was another room, with three beds in it. A man lay fully dressed on top of one of them, snoring. It was Rod.

Gordon's first impulse was to run away. But Rod seemed fast asleep and not immediately dangerous. He hadn't shaved for a day or two, and he was still wearing the black eye-patch that Tony had mentioned. And he had a bruise on his temple and a big, fresh-looking cut in his cheek. As Gordon watched, he muttered something and turned over. Gordon tiptoed from the apartment, then half-ran down the stairs, back along the alley and out through the archway. He had only been in the Shambles five minutes, and as before it had shaken him. It was enough.

He went back thoughtfully to his own home. It was warm and secure, and for the first time he felt that he was lucky. And as the day went on, another feeling grew in him which at first he couldn't recognize because he hadn't had anything quite like it before. It was a feeling of concern. He was worried about Sheila.

Then he remembered that it was Friday, and on Friday afternoons Tony Boyd came to the Vicarage. By four o'clock, Gordon was at the Vicarage door. Tony himself opened it.

'Yes, she's here,' he said at once.

Gordon stared.

'Sheila's here. We brought her here a few nights ago. It seemed the best thing to do.'

'Tony, I don't understand.'

'Come in, Gordon. Come and see her. She's been asking about you. She wanted to send a message, but she seemed afraid of giving secrets away. Your secrets, I mean.'

'Oh yes, the raft and all that,' said Gordon. Puzzled, he stepped inside, wiping his feet carefully on the Vicarage mat. He followed Tony up a staircase, along a corridor and into a largish bedroom, curtained and carpeted and comfortably shabby.

Sheila was in bed, reading. She had a black eye and a bandage round her head, and her face was very white. She smiled, faintly and sheepishly.

'I'm sorry I didn't come,' she said. 'I would have done if I could.'

'That's all right,' he said. 'But what . . .?'

'This is Anne's bedroom,' Sheila said. 'It belongs to Mrs. Wallace's daughter who's at college. Isn't it lovely?'

'Yes, but . . .'

'Mrs. Wallace is ever so kind. And there are hundreds of books. This is a lovely one I'm reading. Called *Moonfleet*. It's about smuggling. That's as exciting as pirating, really. I think Captain Cutlass was probably a smuggler, too, when he wasn't being a pirate.'

'Sheila,' said Tony gently, 'I'd better tell Gordon what happened.'

Sheila turned her face away.

'You don't mind, do you?' Tony said.

'I suppose not,' said Sheila. She concentrated carefully on the book and turned over a page.

'Her uncle had a big fight with Rod the other night,' said Tony.

'What about?' asked Gordon.

'Not about anything in particular. He and Rod don't hit it off. Since Rod was demobbed there's been trouble every night.'

'Not *every* night,' said Sheila, who wasn't really reading. 'Only when they've both been at the *George*.'

'Rod picks a quarrel,' explained Tony. 'Well, you know Rod, Gordon. If he's set on trouble, he'll find a cause for it. And as often as not the cause is Sheila, because she's the odd child out in that family, and her uncle's the only one who cares much about her.'

'And who gave her that black eye? '

'That was Rod,' said Tony. 'He knocked her over a sofa as well.'

Gordon was astonished.

'You mean he hit her? Somebody *his* size hit somebody *her* size?'

'He wouldn't do it any other time,' said Sheila. 'Other times he's all right, more or less. But when Rod gets mad, like he does with my uncle, he might do anything.'

'I saw Rod sleeping on top of the bed just now, with his clothes on,' said Gordon.

'Yes. He threw the uncle out,' said Tony. 'But I believe he took a bit of punishment himself.'

The Vicar had come quietly into the room while this conversation was going on.

'I think we should spare Gordon the details of all this,' he said. 'And spare Sheila having to go through it all again. To cut it short, Gordon, it was a nasty business and there was no telling what might happen next. The mother and the young children were taken into a Corporation mothers-and-babies home. But Mrs. Wallace and I suggested that Sheila should come here for a while.'

'Luckily,' said Tony, 'there's nothing wrong with her except what you can see. We were a bit worried in case she'd hurt herself inside when she went over the sofa. But Dr. Sampson says she's all right. She'll be up and about tomorrow. And staying at the Vicarage all week, I hope.'

A slow indignation had been working its way to the surface of Gordon's mind.

'But it's not right,' he said. 'Getting knocked about at her age. If she isn't safe in her own home, where *is* she safe?'

'They don't really mean to do it,' said Sheila. 'Even Rod. It's only when he gets his temper up.'

'He ought to be in prison,' said Gordon with conviction.

'Oh, no!' said Sheila, shocked. 'Not Rod in prison!'

'None of these things are ever simple,' said Mr. Wallace. 'We're doing our best, along with the Welfare people, to sort this one out. You see, Gordon, an awful lot of people in the district would be in trouble if a strict view was taken of everything that goes on. You ask Sergeant Hawkins. So what the various authorities have to do is turn a blind eye most of the time, just so as to keep life moving along. Specially in these family affairs. If you send a man to prison, you've lost.'

'Sounds to me as if Rod'll be sending somebody to hospital,' said Gordon, 'if he isn't got out of the way.'

'It's a big risk to take,' said Mr. Wallace. He sighed. 'In my job, and in this place, you live by taking risks. Anyway, now you know why Sheila didn't come to see you.'

'We'll finish it ... you know, the Quest ... when I'm about again,' said Sheila.

'Maybe,' said Gordon. Sheila's dream world seemed unimportant now beside the harsh realities of her life.

'Time to be moving on, young man,' said the Vicar. 'You can come again tomorrow if you like. And the day after that I dare say she'll be coming to see *you*.'

'If his mum and dad'll let me,' said Sheila.

CHAPTER 13

Gordon couldn't decide whether to tell his parents or not. He found it hard to guess the effects of some kinds of news. If a child got beaten up at home, did this make her even more undesirable in the eyes of respectable people? He didn't know. But he found he couldn't keep the story to himself. And in fact Sidney and Elsie Dobbs, who were kind enough people in their different ways, were shocked and anxious about Sheila. Next day Gordon was on his way to the Vicarage with an invitation for her to come to tea on the first afternoon she could go out.

She was delivered by the Vicar in person, in his elderly Alvis. She was perfectly clean, having had a daily bath under Mrs. Wallace's supervision. Her hair had been washed. She had on a cotton frock, faded but spotless, that had been worn many years before by Anne Wallace. Small, thin, composed, with neat precise gestures—Gordon could see that she was making a good impression on his mother. If only she'd *belonged* to the Vicarage, what a suitable playmate she'd have been. . . .

After tea Mrs. Dobbs set them playing ludo—a game that bored Gordon but that gave Sheila scope for all kinds of imaginary pursuits and adventures. She grew almost feverishly excited, hurrahing every time she threw a six. And when Mrs. Dobbs left them by themselves in the room, she burst out,

'I'm staying in the pirate's house!'

Gordon supposed he oughtn't to be sarcastic just now, but he couldn't help it.

'Three cheers for Captain Cutlass!' he said. 'Have you found a skull and crossbones under the bed?'

'Don't be silly!' she said. But her eyes grew distant. 'It's lovely there. Full of books and history. I bet it's got secrets written on every brick!'

'Pull a few out and read them,' suggested Gordon. And then, 'Have you found a treasure map?'

'No . . . well, I don't know . . . well, perhaps . . . Yes, I'm sure there's a map. . . . Oh, I'm forgetting my turn!'

She rattled the dice in the cup, threw a six, crowed with delight, threw another six and then a five.

'Seventeen at one turn!' she cried. 'Scudding along in the Roaring Forties!'

The success stimulated her still further.

'There *was* a map!' she said. 'In a panel behind the picture in Anne Wallace's bedroom. Old and yellow and crumbling away at the edges. . . . Your turn, Gordon, you need a four to get your first man home. Oh, it's a five. You only need a one now.'

'And what was on this map?' asked Gordon. 'Blimey, you've thrown another six!' Sheila laughed triumphantly as she moved her counter along the board.

'An island, of course!' she said. 'Pirate's Island! Just think of it, Gordon, exactly like the one we saw, but before the canal came. With palm-trees and blue sky and golden sands. . . .'

'Here, half a minute!' Gordon protested. 'There couldn't be golden sands on a map!'

'There could, there could! It said "Golden sands". Oh, Gordon, you don't seem to be throwing anything but twos. I'm going to beat you!'

'And where is this map?' demanded Gordon.

'It—it crumbled away at a touch. There was nothing left but a little heap of dust. . . . One, two, three, four, five. That's my last man coming along now, Gordon, running before a fair wind. Go on, see if you can throw a six. *Wish* it to be a six. Oh, look, you have!'

'There aren't any golden sands on the island we saw,' said Gordon. 'And there aren't any palm-trees and blue skies in Cobchester.'

'It was different then,' said Sheila. 'In Captain Cutlass's time. Long long ago. And there were birds of paradise in brilliant plumage.'

'Where *they* on the map, too? '

Sheila missed the sarcasm.

'No, you can't show birds on a map,' she said. 'He mentioned them in the letter.'

'Oh, there was a letter as well?'

'Yes. I only have to throw a three to win.'

'Did the letter crumble to dust as well? '

'Yes. It was so old, you see. So fragile, after all those years. As soon as you touched it, it turned to powder.'

'Paper isn't as fragile as that.'

'It was in a story I read. Anyway, this was parchment. Anyway, whatever it was, it crumbled to dust, so you can't see it now. . . . Oh, Gordon, a three! I've won, I've won!'

She bounced on her chair with delight.

'Let's go tomorrow after tea!' she cried. 'To the island, Gordon. To the island!'

'Are you well enough?'

'Of course I am.'

'And will they let you go out?'

'They will if I say I'm going to play with you. It won't be untrue. You can call for me.'

But as she spoke the excitement seemed to be ebbing away from her, and reaction setting in.

'I don't know where I am,' she said. 'I don't know where I am at all.'

She looked at him with bewilderment in her eyes. Suddenly she was crying.

CHAPTER 14

By Monday Sheila had recovered her spirits. She was waiting for Gordon when he arrived at the Vicarage after tea. He'd learned from his previous trips to Gumble's Wharf, and was now wearing a warm coat. Sheila was well wrapped up, too. In his pocket Gordon had put an electric torch, in case it began to get dark before they were back. And on the lid of the biscuit-tin in which he carried food from the shop, he'd scrawled the words *pirates' provisions*.

Sheila objected mildly. 'We're not pirates,' she said. But Gordon was pleased with his handiwork, and added to it a drawing of a ship flying a Jolly Roger as big as itself.

On the way down the canal they overtook a small, spry figure in a blue serge suit. It was Mr. Kite, and he seemed to be in a talkative mood.

'Been to the Old Folks' Tea,' he said. 'Every Monday they have it in the Church Rooms in Lotus Walk. Mrs. Wallace runs it. Very nice, too. It costs fourpence, mind, but it's worth it. Do you know what you get?'

77

The children shook their heads.

'A ham sandwich and a tomato sandwich and a bun and a cup of tea. Not bad, eh? Not bad for fourpence. And you don't even have to pay that if you can't afford it. But I pay, of course. While ever I have my savings I'll pay my way. I have my pride, you know. I have my pride.... And what are you two doing down here?'

'We're taking our raft out,' said Gordon.

'*Hispaniola*,' said Sheila.

'Oh, yes, the raft. I remember. Well, have a good trip. And be careful. You only live once. You've a long way to go till you reach my age, eh? Don't take any risks. Good-bye to you, now.'

Mr. Kite left them and climbed up to his home. He was surprisingly nimble for an old man. The children went round to the shed and eased *Hispaniola* out from the pile of lumber.

Gordon was just closing the shed door behind them when there was a shout and a clatter of feet on the iron staircase. And Mr. Kite came dashing up.

'It's gone!' he cried. 'My chest! My money! Gone!'

They followed him up to the attic.

'Look!' he said. 'That's where I keep it. Behind the washstand there, in the corner. I went to check it just now, like I always do when I come in. And it's gone!'

'Perhaps you put it somewhere else and forgot,' suggested Gordon.

'Impossible! I never put it anywhere else!'

All the same, the old man began rummaging furiously. He moved his bed out from the wall, looked behind it, moved it back, shifted his few other bits of furniture. But there was no sign of the chest. If it had been there it couldn't have stayed hidden for long.

Mr. Kite's expression became one of panic.

'There's all I possess in there!' he said. 'A hundred and eleven pounds, twelve and six. That's my independence. That's my security. That's all there is between me and the workhouse!'

Suddenly he looked suspicious.

'*You've* been hanging about down here!' he said. 'And you were interested in the chest, weren't you? I remember. Oh, yes, I remember. And now all this raft business.'

He paused, then rapped out,

'What's in that tin you've got there?'

Silently Gordon opened his biscuit-tin. It contained pies and sausage rolls and a carton of potted meat.

'If we'd taken your money we wouldn't have come back here afterwards, would we?' he said.

'No. No. Quite true. Don't know what I'm saying, do I? Getting old.' Mr. Kite's cheeks crumpled.

'We could look in the shed, and round about outside,' suggested Gordon without much hope.

But there was no signs of the chest or money anywhere near Gumble's Yard.

Gordon pushed the raft back into the shed. The voyage to Pirate's Island would have to be put off again. It was impossible to start it this evening, after what had happened.

'You'll have to call the police,' he said.

The old man was reluctant.

'Don't like bringing those fellows in,' he said. 'Never know where it'll stop, do you? I don't want folks arrested. I'm too old for going to court and giving evidence. All I want is to get my money back. It can't have gone far in an afternoon.'

'Well, suppose I fetch the Vicar?' Gordon suggested.

This idea seemed more acceptable.

'Oh aye. Mr. Wallace'll do something. Clears folk's troubles up wonderfully, he does. You go for him right away.'

Gordon went. Sheila sat, small and quiet, in a corner of Mr. Kite's room. The old man still couldn't believe that the chest had really gone. He kept jumping up and hunting frantically around, looking again and again in the same places. But at last he gave up and seated himself on the bed, opposite Sheila.

'There's no fool like an old fool,' he said. 'I should have left it in the bank. The Vicar himself said so. But I knew best. You're thinking what an old fool I am, aren't you? Aren't you, eh? Aren't you?'

He sounded almost fierce. Sheila licked her lips nervously and said nothing. Then the old man's strength went out of him, quite suddenly. He sat looking white, drained, shrunken—every day of his age. After a minute his head began to fall forward on his chest. Sheila realized that he was going to sleep. Soon he was in an uneasy doze, shaking his head and muttering angrily from time to time.

CHAPTER 15

'The Vicar's just gone out,' said Tony Boyd. He went into town in Dr. Sampson's car, to a committee meeting. He won't be back an hour. But I'm here, as you can see. What can I do for you, Gordon?'

Gordon told him about Mr. Kite's money. Tony whistled ruefully.

'You'd better come in,' he said. And, when they were in his room,

'Got any ideas on the subject?'

'Yes,' said Gordon. 'Walter Thompson.'

'I'm afraid so,' said Tony. 'It's all too obvious, isn't it? He got Mr. Kite to take his money out of the bank, he knew where the old chap kept it, he waited till he was out at the Old Folks' Tea, and then he took his chance.'

'If the police are called in, they'll soon be on to it,' said Gordon.

'They will indeed,' Tony agreed. And then,

'This is going to hurt Cliff and Betty Thompson, as if they hadn't enough to worry about already with a sick child. . . . Look, there's still just a faint chance. Suppose we can find Walter before the police are called. He'll realize he can't get away with it, and he might give the money back, quick.'

'Well, Mr. Kite doesn't want the police brought in,' said Gordon. 'He only wants to get his savings back. What bothers me about Walter is that it seems *too obvious*. You'd think he'd realize that he'd be the first person to be suspected. He's not so dim as all that.'

'Anyway, it's worth trying,' said Tony. 'It's just possible that we might find him at his own place, in Orchid Grove. It's on our way down to Mr. Kite's, so if Walter isn't in we won't have lost any time. And we can save a few minutes anyway, because the Alvis is outside and I know where there's a spare ignition key. The Vicar won't mind if I use it.'

It took them only a minute to get to Orchid Grove. Betty Thompson answered the door. And they were surprised when she told them that Walter was in, and had been in all day.

'He's not been too well,' she said. 'But he's just getting up now.'

Inside they found Walter in shirt and trousers, unshaven, his hands cupped round a mug of tea.

'Walt,' said Tony, coming straight to the point, 'you know you persuaded old Mr. Kite to take his money out of the bank. Well, he did. And it's vanished.'

'Has it?' said Walter, in a tone of extreme surprise.

'Do you know anything about it?'

'I do not.' Walter was indignant. 'Cliff and Betty were on to me the other day about old man Kite's money, and I told them, it's nowt to do with me. You want to watch what you're saying, young Tony.'

But it seemed to Gordon that there was something about the indignation that didn't ring quite true.

'Anyway, when did all this happen?' Walter asked.

'This afternoon. Only an hour or two ago. He had the money in a chest, and he went to the Old Folks' Tea, and when he came back it was gone.'

'Well, then,' said Walter, a note of triumph in his voice, 'I can prove it wasn't me. Because I've been in bed all day until just ten minutes ago. That's right, isn't it, Betty?'

'That's right,' agreed Betty.

'And you haven't been away from the house, have you, Betty?'

'No, Walt,' said Betty.

'And what's more,' said Walter, 'just in case somebody might think Betty was covering up for me, I can tell you there's been chaps digging up the street outside all day, and they'd have seen me if I'd been out. And the insurance man came about an hour ago and passed the time of day. And what's more again, anyone who likes can search this house from top to bottom and they won't find no chests, or money either. And you can put that in your pipe and smoke it!'

There was a general silence. Walter was obviously pleased with himself.

'I've got what they call an alibi,' he said. 'A cast-iron alibi. And it's just as well, or I'd be having this job pinned on me double quick.'

'You know something about it, all the same!' said Tony sharply.

'I know nowt and I'm saying nowt,' said Walter, 'and there's not a thing that anyone can do.'

'I expect it was Rod Ridgeway,' remarked Gordon.

Just for a split second there was a sign of alarm in Walter's face. But he recovered almost at once.

'You be careful what you say about Rod,' he told Gordon. 'Rod doesn't like having himself talked about. And if Rod doesn't like what you do, he can be nasty. You know that already, don't you, Porky Dobbs?'

'I'll tell you something, Walter,' said Tony. 'It's only a few days since the old man drew the money from the bank. They'll still have a record of the numbers of the notes. Anyone who starts passing them will be picked up.'

This time Walter's confidence was clearly shaken.

'They don't write down the numbers of little amounts like this that they pay over the counter,' he said.

'Little?' said Gordon. A hundred and eleven pounds seemed plenty to him.

'Oh yes they do,' said Tony, replying to Walter. 'Whoever it was that did this, once he tries to spend the money he's as good as standing in the dock. And if it's Rod, they'll be after him anyway. Listen, Walt, let me tell you what I'm going to do. I'm going down to Gumble's Yard to fetch Mr. Kite to the Vicarage, and then we shall wait for Mr. Wallace to come in. We'll probably have to wait the best part of an hour. And if the person who's got this money has any sense, he'll bring it round to the Vicarage during that time, and put it on the doorstep, and ring the bell good and hard, and then make himself scarce. And I dare say that'll be the end of the matter.'

'You make me laugh,' said Walter. But he wasn't laughing. He seemed uneasy now. He swallowed. 'Well,' he said, 'when you came I was just getting ready to go out. Can't stop here talking. Betty, where's my boots?'

'Just going to warn Rod, are you?' said Gordon.

'Never mind that, Gordon,' said Tony. 'Walt can go where he likes. I only hope that in the next hour Mr. Kite's money will turn up.'

'Now look here,' said Walter. 'You've been free with your advice, young Tony. Let me give you some advice. If you know what's good for you, you'll go home and mind your own business and keep your mouth shut. Because if you don't, you might get such a bashing your mother won't recognize you. I'm not threatening you, mind. I'm just giving you a word of friendly warning. And another thing—I'd strongly recommen- you not to follow me now. Understand?'

He was gone. Tony stood up.

'Don't go after him,' Betty Thompson said. 'It's quite right, what he told you. If Rod Ridgeway's mixed up in this, it's best to keep out of it.'

'I wasn't going to go after him,' said Tony. 'I want him to have his chance. It looks as though Rod's got the money— they must have planned the whole thing beforehand—and per- haps they'll decide to do as I suggested and give it back. So let's hope that within the hour the chest will mysteriously reap- pear. If it doesn't, I know what the Vicar will say when he comes in. There's only one thing he *can* say. He'll say the police must be called at once.'

'Let's hope they do put it back, then,' said Betty. She did her best to smile as she showed Tony and Gordon out.

'Well, off we go,' said Tony, feeling in his pocket for the car key. 'Down to Gumble's Yard. Mr. Kite will be wondering what's happened.'

'I'm not coming, Tony,' said Gordon.

'You're not coming? . . . Oh, I see. You've had enough of this affair. Well, I can't blame you, Gordon. It's a tricky business to get involved with. You'd better do as he says. Go home and keep quiet.'

'I didn't mean that . . .' began Gordon. But Tony was already getting into the car. He'd got the wrong idea. Gordon pulled a face. It was a pity Tony should think he was scared, just when he'd decide to do the riskiest thing he'd ever tried in his life. For he didn't believe for one moment that Rod and Walter would meekly return Mr. Kite's property. It seemed to him that this was just the sort of idea that a kind and hopeful and law-abiding person like Tony would have. But Rod and Walter weren't like that. They'd make use of the time they had before the police were called in. They'd hide their booty until it was safe to spend it. And the best hope of getting it back for Mr. Kite was to see what they did with it.

CHAPTER 16

Gordon watched from behind as the Alvis turned out of Orchid Grove and disappeared down Hibiscus Street towards Gumble's Yard. It was dusk now, and Tony had put the sidelights on. Gordon half wished he'd stayed in the car. But it was too late now. He turned the other way and trudged up to Camellia Hill, eastwards along the Wigan Road, and over the railway bridge.

He was heading for the Shambles. Walter, he was sure, had gone straight to Rod. And there was a reasonable chance that Rod would be in that bare deserted apartment where Gordon had seen him the other day.

By the time he reached Slaughter Street it was dark. Over the archway that led into the Shambles, a street lamp came on. Inside there was no light. The moon had not yet risen.

Gordon felt the pains of fear in his stomach. It wasn't good to be in the Shambles after dark. It wasn't good to be looking for Rod, of all people. He told himself he was stupid. All this had nothing to do with him. It wasn't his business that an old man had lost his savings. It wasn't his business that Cliff and Betty Thompson, with a sick child to worry about, would have more worries if Walter got into trouble. Least of all was it his business to get entangled with the man who'd half-wrecked Mr. Dobbs's shop, who'd knocked Sheila over a sofa, who was as violent and dangerous as any man in the Jungle.

Gordon was no hero, and he knew it. But he knew, too, that this was the challenge; this was the moment he'd been moving towards over the last few weeks.

The pool of light from the street lamp stretched a few feet through the archway. A tall unshaven man with a wild look came lurching from somewhere inside, brushed heavily against Gordon without seeming to notice him, and disappeared along Slaughter Street. Gordon decided he didn't like the light anyway—he felt exposed to view. If there was safety now, it was in the dark. He slipped quickly through the archway and into the darkness beyond.

The narrow alley in which he'd found the entrance to Sheila's dwelling was on the left. In the dark he found it difficult to count the number of entries, and wasn't sure when he had gone far enough. A glimmer of light led him through an opening and into a little stone-flagged lobby like the one he'd been in before. But the numbers were wrong. And from somewhere upstairs came sounds of hard swearing, of blows and intermittent wails. He went out quickly, and a few yards along the street found the next entry.

This was the right one. A tiny gas lamp in a high bracket gave just enough light for him to see the ground-floor numbers 15 and 16. The row of dustbins was overflowing. An alley-cat —perhaps the one he'd seen before, perhaps not—foraged in the rubbish.

Gordon hadn't thought beyond this point. He didn't know what he was going to do now. But he supposed he wasn't far behind Walter—if Walter had come here. And if anything was going to happen, it was bound to happen soon.

Luck was with him. He'd hardly found his bearings when he heard voices from the top of the stair that led to No. 17. A quick, light voice—Walter's. A slow, thick one—Rod's. Gordon darted to the other stair, the one that went down to the basement. It was totally dark there. He crept down a few steps and crouched low. Nobody could see him.

Footsteps came shuffling down into the lobby and echoed

from the stone flags. From the instructions muttered to each other, it seemed that Rod and Walter were carrying something. Gordon wasn't surprised. He knew what it would be—the chest with 'C.C.' on it. That chest would take a bit of hiding. He peeped out cautiously to see their backs disappearing from the building into the alleyway, then followed.

Rod and Walter turned left, the opposite way from the archway. They were moving quite fast now. After a few yards they turned from the alley into an even narrower passageway between two buildings. Then they crossed a small courtyard and at the other side of it Gordon almost lost them. But a voice hailed them and asked what they were doing, to be answered by Rod with a snarled 'Shut up!'

They were heading downhill towards the canal, and soon came to another archway in the old wall. It was like the one in Slaughter Street, and had a street lamp over it. Gordon caught a brief glimpse of them—Walter wearing a cap, Rod carrying what looked like a spade, and the black eye-patch showing as his face caught the light. And the chest was slung between them.

They were still hurrying. Now they went down a passageway that skirted the railway on one side and the Canal Company's premises on the other. Gordon went warily after them. And a couple of minutes later the noise of boots on stone setts changed, and the two men were crunching along the gravel of the tow-path.

They had turned right towards the railway viaduct. The tow-path went under it. A goods-train rumbled loudly and slowly overhead, drowning all other sounds. Gordon gave them time to get ahead, then darted for the shelter of the viaduct and peered round one of its supports. In front of him now was the gable end of the row of cottages at Gumble's Yard. He couldn't see Rod or Walter, and thought at first that they'd got away from him. For a minute, two minutes, there was silence. Then there were scraping sounds, a few curses from Rod, a splash. Gordon remembered that Mr. Kite had mentioned a boat in one of the outbuildings, belonging to the Canal Company. Anyone could open that lock, the old man had said. It looked as if Rod and Walter had done so, and got the boat out.

'Leaky as hell!' came Walter's whisper from the water, followed by a 'Wrap up!' from Rod and more curses. Then came the sound of oars, and Gordon made out the lines of a square, clumsy, punt-like vessel, now heading back under the viaduct and eastward along the canal.

He was looking after them, still keeping in the shadow of the viaduct but feeling baffled and beaten, when there was a touch on his arm. It was Sheila.

'What are you doing?' he whispered, startled.

'I knew I'd find you here,' she said.

'You couldn't have done. I didn't know I'd be here myself.'

'Well, I did. So when Tony and Mr. Kite got back to the Vicarage, I pretended I was going to bed. And instead I crept away and came to meet you.'

'But listen,' said Gordon, 'how could you possibly know where I'd be?'

'Because I knew what those two would do. And I knew you'd need the raft to follow them. And I knew you'd need me to help you with the raft.'

'Well, if you know what those two are doing,' said Gordon, 'you know more than I do.'

'Of course I know what they're doing. They're burying the treasure—I mean Mr. Kite's money.'

'Burying it where?' asked Gordon. But even as he spoke he knew what Sheila's answer would be. And wild as it might seem, he knew in his bones that it was correct.

'Pirate's Island,' she said. 'Where else would anybody bury treasure? Pirate's Island, of course.'

CHAPTER 17

The raft, with its makeshift paddles, was still in Mr. Kite's shed. They dragged it out on to the wharf and tipped it over the edge into the canal. Rod and Walter were now out of earshot. Gordon jumped down and, more confident than before, held out his arms for Sheila. In a moment they were safely aboard. They pushed off from the wharf and drifted into mid-canal, then paddled, slowly and awkwardly, the way the two men had gone.

A quarter-mile along, they heard the first sounds, carrying faintly across the water. Undoubtedly Rod and Walter were on the island. And although they were working as quietly as they could, the chink of spade on gravelly soil was unmistakable.

Gordon and Sheila paddled the raft cautiously onwards. They were getting near the Canal Company's main premises, and the first of many inlets was on their left. In better days it had held a dozen barges, and the great iron rings remained. Gordon tied up the raft to the nearest of them, and the children lay flat on their stomachs, watching. With their eyes used to the dark, they could just dimly see the moving shapes of the two men as they dug.

'*You* gave Rod that idea!' Gordon whispered to Sheila. 'Just like you suggested the eye-patch!'

'I might have done,' she admitted. 'I did say, before the—before the trouble, that if ever he wanted to bury treasure he should bring it here. And he told me to shut up or he'd clout me. But Gordon, I didn't suggest he should steal somebody's money.'

Gordon opened his mouth to tell her she ought to have been more careful. Then he reminded himself that this wasn't the time or place for an argument. They both went on silently watching.

Work seemed to go on for a long time. It looked as though the digging was a harder job than Walter and Rod had expected. Whispered comments and curses drifted across the water at intervals. Gordon thought he saw a growing mound of gravel. He thought he saw Rod and Walter swing the chest between them, he thought he heard a thud as it landed in the hole, he thought he saw the mound diminish as gravel was shovelled back into it. He thought he saw and heard both men trampling the place flat. Afterwards he was never quite sure how much of this had been supplied by his imagination. But certainly the chest was buried, and at length Rod and Walter were in their boat again, rowing it gently back along the canal. This time they came nearer the bank, and for a dreadful moment Gordon and Sheila felt sure they'd been seen. But they lay motionless and the boat went past them, back towards the viaduct and Gumble's Yard.

The children stayed where they were for many minutes, giving Rod and Walter time to put the boat back and set off again on foot for the Shambles. Then, cautiously, they edged the raft out into mid-canal and paddled towards the island.

Gordon didn't know or greatly care what excitement Sheila might feel on reaching her island at last. To him (if he'd thought about the matter at all) the indigo brickwork rising its couple of feet out of the water, and the few square yards of sour gritty soil it enclosed, would have seemed a sorry contrast with the coral strands of Sheila's imagination. He had one sole aim—to find where Walter and Rod had dug their hole, and to get its contents out of it as quickly as possible.

He tied up to one of the iron rings and they scrambled-ashore. The moon was rising now, but even so it was impossible without lights to see what part of the surface had been disturbed. Gordon had expected this. He took off his coat and shone the torch from under it, concealing the light as far as possible. And now he could just see the marks where boots had trodden the surface flat. With the help of the rough-and-ready paddles, Gordon and Sheila began to dig. The fact that they could move the soil at all was practical proof that they were in the right place. Anywhere else, they could not have shifted it with the implements they had. Even so, it was a long job, and Gordon grew impatient. Without bothering about torn skin, he started clawing handfuls of dirt and gravel out of the deepening hole. That was how he came to find himself holding something made of cloth. He jerked and tugged until it came out. And when he saw what it was, he groaned.

'Walter's cap!'

'Fancy leaving that,' whispered Sheila, not realizing at first what it meant. 'How ever did it manage to get into the hole?'

'He threw it down while he was digging, I expect,' said Gordon. 'Then when they were filling the hole in the dark, one of them shovelled the cap in with a spadeful of soil. And when they finished, they were in such a hurry to get away that I expect Walter forgot about it.'

'That was careless.'

'But don't you see?' Gordon was impatient. 'By now he'll have realized he hasn't got his cap. And they won't dare to leave it, because for all they know it might be just lying around, giving them away. *They're bound to come back!*'

Sheila said no more, but they dug away frantically with hands and paddles. There was little joy but a great deal of relief when they reached the chest. And it took two or three final panicky minutes to get it clear of the soil and out of the hole.

'Shall we tidy the place up again?' Sheila asked.

'Don't be daft, there isn't time!' hissed Gordon. He was desperate to get away. 'It doesn't matter now. Come on, let's get the chest aboard!'

That wasn't as easy as it seemed, and anxiety didn't help. First Gordon jumped down to the raft. Then he realized that Sheila's arms weren't strong enough to hand the chest down to him. It would be disastrous if they dropped it in the water. He clambered ashore again, helped Sheila descend to the raft, then lay on his stomach on the bank, holding the chest out to her with both hands. She got a grip on the handles but couldn't control the weight, and when Gordon let the chest go it landed at her feet. The raft rocked, water lapped for a moment round the chest, then Sheila dragged it into the safety of the centre section formed by the upturned table. Gordon jumped after it. And at that moment they heard what he'd been dreading ever since he found the cap—the sound of returning oars.

Gordon and Sheila paddled for the canal-bank. Gordon thought they managed to get away before being noticed. But a minute later he heard, across the quiet water, the two men's heavy whispers.

'What's happened, Rod? What's happened? That heap of earth!'

'Whatjermean?'

'We didn't leave it like that. Look, Rod. Someone's been!'

A moment's silence as Rod took it in. Then,

'They flippin' well 'ave! Who could it 'a' been, Walt? There's nobody there now.'

'Can't have gone far, Rod. There hasn't been time.'

'If I catch 'em, I'll . . .'

Gordon shuddered. And the next words were more frightening still.

'Listen! Rod! Over there. Listen! I can hear them.'

He signalled to Sheila to stop paddling. In the dark it was still just possible to hope that they wouldn't be seen. But next moment they heard the splash of oars as the boat came after them, a good deal less quietly now.

They were approaching the Canal Company's main wharf. Gordon never knew exactly how he got ashore or dragged up the chest. He had a vague recollection afterwards of a desperate moment when he pulled Sheila after him, the raft moved away from under her feet, and he thought he would lose her in the canal's black water. But it all happened too quickly for fright. They were running away, the chest between them, before the boat reached the wharf. Rod, no longer bothering to keep quiet, was shouting threats at them.

A group of deserted warehouses made up part of the Canal Company's premises. Gordon and Sheila ran round the side of the first of these. But even in their panic they realize that they couldn't hope to get away while they were carrying that chest. At the back of the warehouse was a stack of what might have been crates, covered with tarpaulin. Without conscious thought, almost without stopping, they shoved the chest under a corner of the tarpaulin and ran on.

They crossed an open space and ran round the side of another building. As they did so, the sound of boots came from behind them. One of the men—it must be Walter—was ashore and chasing them. He was gaining, too. Gordon was no great runner and felt puffed already. Sheila, lighter and quicker, could have got away easily but seemed to be going slowly to stay with him. At the next corner Gordon seized her hand and drew her beside him, flat against a warehouse wall. The footsteps came nearer, slowed down, stopped a few feet away. There was a moment's pause, during which Gordon tried desperately to silence his own gulpings for breath. Then came a low call from somewhere behind. Walter, if it was Walter, turned back. The children ran on, at right angles to their original direction.

Seconds later, they stopped suddenly at the brink of more water. The wharves, buildings and canal inlets formed a maze, and they were in the middle of it in the dark. Soon they lost any clear sense of where they were going, but they blundered on, hearing no more of Rod or Walter, and watching mostly for their own safety.

And then they came out on the edge of the railway sidings. The three or four nearest tracks were empty, but beyond them stood a long line of wagons. Gordon and Sheila stumbled across the rails towards them. All had high sides. Gordon's instinct was to get into them and hide, but he couldn't see how they'd climb up. Then, as he looked, something happened inside his head—his panic lifted like a fog, his mind was clear, and for the first time since leaving the water he was able to think.

There was no sign of Rod or Walter. They must have given up the chase. What were they doing, then? The answer was plain enough. They were looking for the chest, realizing that the children must have put it down soon after leaving the raft. And it wouldn't take them long to find it, for the hiding-place, if you could call it that, was an obvious one.

He whispered to Sheila. Cautiously the children set off back towards the main wharf. The railway tracks gave them a sense of direction, and they found their way without too much trouble. Soon, creeping round the edge of a dump of old iron, they saw in front of them the open space they'd crossed to reach the first warehouse. And they could just see, and just hear, Rod and Walter groping about, complaining and cursing. They hadn't yet looked round the corner where the pile of crates lay covered with tarpaulin. But any moment they would do so, and the chest would be found.

Gordon's boot touched a loose half-brick. And as it did so, an idea came to him. He picked up the brick, then whispered in Sheila's ear. They made their way, under the lee of the nearest shed, to a point where the tarpaulined crates were opposite them and the heap of old iron was on their right. The main wharf, where Rod and Walter had left their boat, was thirty or forty yards to the left. Gordon hesitated for a moment, frightened by the big risk he was going to take. But by now he was getting used to feeling scared. If you couldn't be brave, he'd found, you could just admit to yourself that you were scared, and then carry on regardless. And even as he paused he saw Rod come round the warehouse corner and bend as if to lift that tarpaulin. With all his strength, Gordon hurled the half-brick towards the top of the heap of iron.

In the quiet of the deserted wharves, the noise it made was shattering. The brick bounced down the pile, dislodging pieces of metal on the way, knocking one thing into another, banging and thudding and clattering. And the sounds were multiplied as they echoed to and from between the buildings.

'Them kids!' called Walter. And both men dashed towards the source of the noise.

This was the children's chance. Sheila raced for the boat, jumped in and untied it. Gordon made for the pile of crates. He thought he knew exactly where the chest was. But he'd misjudged it, and had to fumble while precious seconds passed. And when he did find it, he had to carry it by himself, held awkwardly in front of him with both arms.

The men hadn't noticed him yet. They were still searching around the junk-heap. But no more concealment was possible. Burdened with the chest, Gordon lumbered as best he could towards the quay. He was half-way there when he heard fresh shouting from Rod and Walter, followed by the ring of footsteps on stone setts. He didn't look round but managed with a desperate effort to increase his pace. Even so, the pursuer—it must be Walter—was catching up with him rapidly.

Gasping for breath, heart thudding, Gordon lurched on. The edge of the wharf, the water, the boat appeared in front of him. He flung the chest forward and followed it, landing on top

94

of it in the boat and setting up a wild rocking. Between boat and wharf a gap opened. Gordon righted himself as Sheila pushed off. And then Walter was on the quay, was looming over them. He jumped. The boat was moving. By a split second, by an inch or two, Walter missed. There was a scraping of boots on wood, a flurry of clothing, a great splash, and then a head appeared above water and hands gripped the gunwale.

Gordon picked up the chest once more and brought it hard down on Walter's knuckles. Walter squealed and loosed his grip. The hands vanished. A moment later, the boat was four or five yards out into the canal while Rod, on the bank, was clumsily dragging Walter ashore and bawling names at him as he did so.

CHAPTER 18

When the children were afloat again, the tension that had kept
them going seemed suddenly to fail them. They grew clumsy,
getting in each other's way. The oars were in the bottom of
the boat, but it was a couple of minutes before they were or-
ganized and Gordon was ready to start rowing.

They weren't out of trouble by any means. On the far bank
of the canal was a high smooth wall that couldn't possibly be
climbed. A road ran along the top of it, following the canal
for three or four miles. There was no way out there. On the
near bank was the Canal Company's wharf, occupied by Rod
and Walter, both of whom would now be in a more dangerous
mood than ever. Westward the towpath ran under the viaduct
to Gumble's Yard and beyond—but Rod and Walter could
move along it much faster than Gordon could row, and wherever he landed they'd be waiting for him. Eastward, toward
the city centre, were high walls again for as he could see. There
was no sign of any landing-place, but neither was there a tow-
path. At least if he went along there he'd get away from the

two men.

Gordon put the boat about and rowed eastward. As he did so, he remembered the raft. Would Rod and Walter attempt to use it? He rather hoped they would. Even if it would hold them, it would be far outstripped by the boat, and he would have a better chance of getting safely ashore. At the moment they didn't even seem to be considering it. They were standing together at the water's edge, Walter still dripping, Rod shaking his fist, and neither of them bothering to keep their remarks quiet.

The boat left them behind. Now it was in a canyon, walled in at both sides. It was darker along here, and cold. Sheila was trembling. And then Gordon heard the sounds of falling water, saw a black opening in the northern wall of the canal, and remembered the River Midwell. Here was the place where he and Sheila, a couple of weeks ago, had looked down from above to see the river's end as it splashed its last few feet down from the tunnel to lose itself in the canal.

Beside the tunnel's mouth was a railed inspection platform, three or four feet square. It was approached from the water by a flight of a dozen steps. At the foot of the steps was a mooring-ring. Gordon headed for this and tied up.

'What are you going to do?' Sheila asked.

'I don't know. . . . I just wondered. . . . Well, it's one way out. Help me with the chest.'

They dragged the chest up the steps and put it on the platform between them. Neither said a word, but now Sheila knew what Gordon intended.

'I'll try it first,' he said.

He edged his way awkwardly from the platform into the mouth of the tunnel. The weather had been dry lately, and the water flow was fairly slight. The 'river' was only five or six inches deep, even in the middle, and at each side of it the bare, slippery concrete was exposed.

'All right,' he called to Sheila, able at last to use his voice without risk. Her thin arms could hardly lift the chest, but she managed to pass it to him and he put it safely down by the water's edge inside the tunnel. Sheila followed, and with a shoulder braced against the rough brickwork Gordon pulled her round the corner to crouch beside him.

Where the roof of the tunnel was highest they could just stand upright, but that meant putting both feet in the water. Gordon, long past caring about wet feet, decided to try it. But the bed of the tunnel was slimy and the water-pressure stronger than he'd expected. It would be all too easy to lose your footing and be swept as if by a water-chute down into the canal. At the sides, the surface was still slippery but not so dangerously so, and you could feel for handholds along the wall as you went. But it meant bending almost double.

Gordon and Sheila slung the chest between them once more and set off along the tunnel, one at each side of the stream. There was a slight upward slope, but that was nothing much. It was not being able to straighten up that made their progress so painful. And after a few yards the darkness closed in. The patch of light behind them, where they'd entered the tunnel, soon dwindled. The far end was up in Claypits, where the river went underground, and that was a good mile away. The blackness was deeper than anything Gordon had ever known. He felt it like a woolly bandage over his eyes. He felt, too, the weight of all that earth above, laden with roads and railway lines and buildings, pressing down on him. He had a sudden terror of being buried alive.

He remembered the torch, still in his coat-pocket, and called to Sheila to stop. Taking a hand off the wall, he groped for the torch, switched it on, and transferred it to the hand that already held one end of the chest. It was awkward to manage, but he had to keep the other hand to guide himself. They trudged on for perhaps a quarter-mile, a little cheered by the light. And then Gordon slipped, went down full length, and dropped the torch in the water. In its rubber casing it floated easily. Before he could make a grab for it, it was out of reach. They watched it, still shining, as it was carried downstream away from them and out of sight. And all was total blackness again—blacker, it seemed, than ever.

'Never mind,' Gordon said. 'We'll soon be out of it now.' Sheila said nothing, and above the sound of the water he heard nothing, but a sixth sense, called into being by the dark, told him she was sobbing quietly as she walked. A minute later something ran over his foot. He thought it was a rat, and wondered how many more there were. Suppose there were hundreds gathering round, ready to attack them? But if there were, wouldn't he see hundreds of pairs of eyes, shining? He could see no eyes. He could see nothing. The sound of water, the slippery concrete underfoot, the rough brick wall that had torn his hand already, the weight of the chest on the other arm, the knowledge of Sheila invisible at the other end of it—these were his world now. He was cramped from all the bending, but it was impossible to sit or lie and there was no point in trying to rest standing up. The only thing was to keep moving.

Gordon lost any sense of time or distance, and half lost consciousness. He plodded on automatically, clothes wet, muscles aching. How Sheila kept going he could not guess and didn't care to think about. He found that a few words she'd spoken the first time they met were going through his mind, with heavy emphasis as he planted each foot ahead of him. *To*pazes and *cin*namon and *gold* moi*dores*. *To*pazes and *cin*namon and *gold* moi*dores*. Topazes were jewels. Cinnamon was a spice. He didn't know what moidores were, but they sounded like Spanish coins. A chest of moidores. The chest they were carrying had no moidores in it, but it had pounds and ten-shillingses and half-crowns belonging to Mr. Kite. . . . Unless Rod and Walter had taken them out. What if it was empty? But it couldn't be empty. When they were on the canal he'd heard it rattle. There must be coins there at least. Or stones? What if he and Sheila were doing all this for a mere box with a few worthless pebbles in it?

He felt Sheila stumble. He felt the far end of the chest dip, felt it dragged down and backwards away from him. He braced himself, took the strain, luckily didn't slip. And then he felt it right itself. She'd recovered her footing. The chest had been her lifeline. Gordon still said nothing. There was no point in saying anything. They only had to go on, and go on. Topazes and cinnamon and gold moidores. Topazes and cinnamon and gold moidores. He began to wonder if they were in the wrong tunnel, if this one didn't come out in Claypits after all. It felt as if it had gone on for miles, would go on for ever. Topazes and cinnamon. . . .

'It's getting lighter, Gordon!' she cried after another minute. 'It's getting lighter!' And it was. It wasn't black any more, it was only dark. But he didn't feel any surge of joy, any sudden energy. He was past that. He just kept going. Topazes and cinnamon and gold moidores. A patch of light came into view. It was the top end of the tunnel. It was getting bigger. Topazes and cinnamon. They were moving into it now. And gold moidores. It was right ahead of them, it was only moonlight, but it was like day after what lay behind. Topazes and cinnamon and ... Gordon's boots squelched into mud. There was no concrete any more. He was standing in the ooze of the River Midwell, where people threw their old tyres and oil-drums. He was in the open air. The tunnel lay behind. It was nothing but a black opening, a sound, a smell, a memory. Beside him, wet, drooping, covered in all kinds of filth, was Sheila. Between them still was the chest. A fine rain was falling on his face.

Gordon came quickly to his full senses. He didn't know how long they'd been in the tunnel, but it felt like a long time. Rod and Walter could have left the wharves, could have followed along the canal-bank, could have seen the boat moored by the tunnel, could even now be heading up through the Jungle to cut them off.

'Come on, come on!' he called to Sheila. It was cruel, for she seemed hardly able to stand, but she responded. They climbed the grass bank and squeezed through the gap in the fence into Midwell Street. Gordon had once been stuck in this gap, but tonight, not minding whether he tore his clothes, he got through easily. And now they ran downhill through the rain, splashing carelessly through puddles, still frightened but at the same time joyful at being out in the open and not buried alive. They crossed the Wigan Road, with a mere hundred yards of Camellia Hill between them and the safety of the Vicarage. Gordon felt triumph rising within him.

It was then that a motor-cycle roared up from Hibiscus Street, seemed to be heading straight at them, stopped short by a few yards with headlamp full on. Walter jumped from the back of it before it stopped, was blocking their way, was shouting something. They ran forward faster still, swung the chest instinctively together, knocked him straight back and into the gutter. The Vicarage was thirty yards away, twenty, fifteen. The motor-cycle clattered to the ground where Rod had dropped it. His running footsteps were behind them. Ten yards, five. The Vicarage door opened to the knob. They were in. Rod was in, too, not giving up even now. Along a corridor another door was open. It was Mr. Wallace's study and he was at the telephone. Tony Boyd and Mr. Kite were with him. Wet and dirty, with torn clothes, the children lurched in, dropped the chest on the floor with a crash. Rod came through the door after them. And now at last he thought better of it. Before the Vicar and Tony could move towards him, he was gone.

100

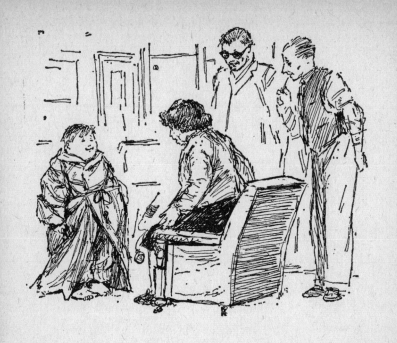

CHAPTER 19

Gordon was delivered to his parents later that evening. He arrived in the Vicar's Alvis, wearing a pair of Mr. Wallace's pyjamas rolled up at sleeves and ankles and a dressing-gown that trailed on the floor. The Vicar had a story to tell that alarmed Mrs. Dobbs but brought grunts of surprised satisfaction from her husband.

'I always knew the lad had something in him,' Mr. Dobbs said afterwards, when the Vicar had gone and Gordon was in bed. 'You've spoiled him, that's all. It made me sick to see him, mooning about and eating all the time. What he needed was to get outside a bit and stand on his own feet.'

'Oh, you're hopeless, Sidney Dobbs,' said his wife. 'Always were and always will be. It's no good talking to you.'

It had struck Mrs. Dobbs at once that Gordon's adventure might have had a much less happy outcome. It was all very well, she thought, for her husband to be full of approval when it was all over and they knew that Gordon hadn't come to any harm. But she'd still have preferred the lad not to take any risks. And she had a feeling that he was slipping out of her grip, that he'd never be quite the same again.

Still, the Vicar had given a glowing account of his exploits, and had invited Gordon to tea at the Vicarage next day. That was something to be pleased about. She tiptoed into Gordon's room before she went to bed, and looked with pride at his sleeping face. He was a fine boy. Mr. Wallace had said so.

Gordon had fallen asleep as once, and slept heavily for a time. Then he became restless, and dreamed again and again of tramping through tunnels and being pursued by Rod, waking each time as Rod's grip closed on his shoulder. In the morning he was flushed, and had a temperature and a slight sore throat. By midday it was clear that he had a bad, feverish cold. He spent the next few days in bed. It was nearly a week before he finally arrived—sitting in the van beside his father, and carrying a present of pies and sausage-rolls—for the promised Vicarage tea.

Gordon was glad to see that Sheila was there, and apparently still staying at the Vicarage. But she didn't eat much, only picking at her food. The Vicar and his wife didn't eat much either, for one of the practices that Mrs. Wallace had carefully kept up through ten years in the Jungle was that of having evening dinner rather than high tea. But Tony had a healthy appetite, and Gordon, recovering after a week in which he hadn't felt much like eating, astonished everyone by the amounts he put away.

Sheila looked reproachfully at him as he reached for his third cream-cake.

'I have to keep my strength up,' he said. He was echoing, as often before, his mother's words. But he felt independent all the same, and felt three inches taller since last week.

And his curiosity needed satisfying as much as his appetite. When he and Sheila had arrived at the Vicarage with the chest the week before, they'd been so wet and dirty that Mrs. Wallace had hustled them both off at once for baths. Then he'd had to change and had been driven straight home and put to bed, and he hadn't been out of his own house since. He wanted to know what had happened.

'Was Mr. Kite's money really in the chest?' he asked first.

'Yes, indeed,' Mr. Wallace said. 'The chest was locked and Mr. Kite's had the key. And although of course Rod and Walter would eventually have forced it open, they hadn't done so. We think Rod must have agreed that he wouldn't open it till Walter came, so that Walter could be sure he was getting his fair share. And when Walter did come, there wasn't time. They had to go straight out and hide it.'

'Did you put the police on to them?'

'No. I was just trying to get through to Sergeant Hawkins on the telephone when you arrived. But as soon as Mr. Kite found his money was safe, he wouldn't hear of a prosecution. And at his age—well, we didn't feel we could force him. He went straight to the bank next morning and put the money back in again. I gather he spent quite a while apologizing to them for doubting their financial soundness. And so far as he's concerned, that's the end of the matter. He's learned his lesson the hard way, and he doesn't want to be troubled about it any more.'

'And Rod and Walter?'

'Nobody knows what's happened to them. They've made themselves scarce for the time being. They haven't been seen since that night. But the general view is that they'll turn up before long like a pair of bad pennies.'

'Tell Gordon about the chest,' said Sheila.

'Oh, yes. Well, after what had happened, Mr. Kite took a dislike to it. He said he didn't want it sitting around reminding him what a silly old man he'd been. So we brought it back from him for the same price as he'd paid. It's in my study now.'

'Funny, isn't it,' said Tony, 'how the chest went full circle? After all those years in the attic here, it went to Nick Batten's shop, then down to Mr. Kite's at Gumble's Yard, then over to the Shambles, then by water to the island in the canal—'

'Pirate's Island,' said Sheila.

'Pirate's Island,' Tony agreed. 'Then to the Canal Company's wharves, then on the water again, then up through the tunnel and finally back to the Vicarage.'

'Well, this is where it belongs,' said Sheila solemnly.

'I'd no business to let it go,' said Mrs. Wallace.

'Then why . . .?' began Gordon. But he felt a sharp kick on the ankle. Sheila was warning him off that subject. He broke off in mid-sentence and said instead,

'I'd like to have another look at it if I could.'

The chest had been scarred during its travels, but Tony and Sheila between them had cleaned and polished it lovingly, and it seemed very little the worse. Gordon looked at it with some awe, then raised the lid.

'You won't find one,' said Sheila.

'Find one what?' said Gordon.

But he knew what she meant, and she knew that he knew. He thought there might be a secret compartment, undiscovered all these years. He felt every inch of the surface, inside and out, then turned the chest upside-down and sideways. And reluctantly he concluded that she was right.

'There's nothing there,' he admitted.

'Oh, I wouldn't say there's nothing there,' said the Vicar. 'No amazing secrets, perhaps. As you get older you stop expecting them. But a very fine chest all the same, a work of craftsmanship. And a work of some historical interest, I dare say. Look as those initials, "C.C.", the same as on the house. I don't know who "C.C." was—'

'Captain Cutlass,' said Sheila.

'—But whoever he was, both chest and house must have been his. The deeds unluckily aren't complete and don't throw any light on him. That's a pity.'

'You know,' said Tony thoughtfully, 'there are proper ways of doing these things. I reckon it would take less than a morning to find out about "C.C." and his house, and maybe his chest. It'd be fun for Gordon and Sheila. And seeing that school starts again on Monday, we'd better do it tomorrow. I'll come for you at ten o'clock, Gordon, and we'll look into it together, all three of us. How's that?'

'Oh, fine,' said Gordon. 'I suppose we'll start by finding the wooden-legged stranger with a black beard . . .'

For the second time he felt a sharp kick under the table.

'What do you mean, Gordon?' asked Tony.

'Nothing,' said Gordon. 'Just a joke. All right, Tony, I'll be with you in the morning.'

CHAPTER 20

Tony called half an hour earlier than expected next day. He was driving the Alvis again, and looked very grown-up.

'I've to go round to Sheila's place,' he told Gordon when they were in the car. 'There are some things I must pick up. And I wanted to have a word with you. We can't be always discussing the poor child in front of herself.'

'What's going to happen to her, Tony?' Gordon asked. 'I keep thinking of her, having to go back to the Shambles.'

'She won't go back to the Shambles any more,' said Tony.

'Then what *will* happen?'

Tony hesitated.

'We oughtn't really to talk about it until the red tape's all been disentangled,' he said. 'The law's involved, and the Child Care people, and I don't know who else. But when it's all been sorted out, Sheila's going to have a new home. Normally, the way these things are looked at nowadays, the authorities don't like to take a child away from its family. The idea is that even a poor home should be kept together if possible. But Sheila's is an exceptional case.'

'Hers is hardly a home at all,' said Gordon.

'Exactly. The welfare people think they can put the family together again, more or less, if Rod will stay away for good. But even if they manage that, Sheila will still be the odd child out. Nobody cares for her, nobody knows what to make of her. That's probably why the authorities agree that she should be moved. And apart from everything else, she's an imaginative, sensitive child, and she hasn't got a chance with that background.'

'Where will she go?' asked Gordon.

'I'll give you one guess.'

'I don't know.'

'Think about it.'

Gordon thought. After a minute he said,

'Not . . . the Vicarage?'

'Yes, of course. Mr. and Mrs. Wallace will adopt her if it all works out. Which I think it will.'

Gordon didn't say anything.

'Isn't that splendid?' Tony asked.

'Yes. Yes. I suppose so,' said Gordon. But he wasn't quite sure. He thought of his own parents who, whatever their faults, cared deeply for him. 'I wouldn't like to be adopted,' he said.

'I think you might if you were in Sheila's position. The thought that bothers me is something quite different. It's this. There just happens to be a way out for Sheila, because we know her and because she's an exceptional person. But how many children are there in this city who aren't any better placed than she is? How many of them can we do anything for? . . . Sorry, Gordon, I mustn't be depressing on a fine morning. And here we are. That archway is the entrance to the Shambles. But I don't need to tell you that, do I, Gordon?'

'No, you don't,' said Gordon grimly.

'I've to collect Sheila's remaining possessions and take them to the Vicarage,' Tony said. 'Are you coming in with me?'

Gordon didn't really want to, but didn't like to refuse. At least, he thought, Tony seemed able to approach the Shambles as if it was just a place like any other place. And indeed, though gloomy enough, the Shambles in today's daylight looked far less sinister than before.

They left the car outside the archway, walked inside, found the entry that led to Sheila's dwelling. Tony knocked at the

106

door, which stood slightly ajar, and then pushed it wide open. Then he stepped back quickly.

'Go back to the car, Gordon,' he said. 'Rod's in there.'

Gordon had found in the last few weeks that he had a good deal of dogged courage when he needed it. But he also had a well-developed streak of caution. He wasn't a boy to look for trouble if he could avoid it. And after the chase round the wharves he didn't want to meet Rod. He didn't really want Tony to come up against Rod either.

'Let's both go,' he whispered, 'and come back another time.'

But Rod had heard them.

'Who's that whisperin' out there?' called the well-known thick voice. 'Come in an' let's 'ave a look at you!'

Tony stepped forward. Gordon followed him.

'Oh. Tony Boyd. An' young Dobbs.'

Rod showed no special interest in Gordon. His mind didn't seem to be on the recent chase at all. He'd stopped wearing the eye-patch.

'Well, I've come back,' he said to Tony.

'So I see, Rod.'

'An' just look at it.' Rod swept an arm round the room in which they stood. It was barer than ever now. There was a broken-down iron bedstead from which mattress and bedding had been removed. There was a sofa with two or three springs sticking out, the small battered rocking-chair in which the little girl had sat, a chest and a few boxes.

'I thought the powers-that-be might 'ave put the 'appy 'ome together again by now,' Rod said. He sounded slightly aggrieved, as if he thought authority had let him down.

'I believe it's you they've been worried about, Rod,' said Tony. 'They were afraid there might be more trouble between you and your stepfather. They didn't want anyone else getting hurt.'

Tony was thin-lipped and nervous. He watched for the dangerous glint that could come so easily to Rod's eye. But Rod seemed subdued this morning.

'Aye, well,' he said, 'I never could get on with 'im. Didn't matter when I was in the Army, but since I been demobbed . . . I don't know what it is, but 'e always says summat to make me mad. And I say summat back to 'im, and 'e says summat more. It's as if we was forced into it. And when I lose my temper, young Tony . . .'

'I know, Rod,' said Tony.

'Maybe it's time I left,' said Rod.

'Well, the Vicar was saying that if you went permanently, the rest of them could move back in. Except Sheila.'

Rod was thoughtful.

'I been thinkin' about it myself,' he said. 'Nowt to do with any flippin' vicars, but I been gettin' fed up around 'ere. I might go back into construction, like I was before I was called up. One o' them big firms, with sites all over the country. It's a hard life, but there's good wages if you've got the strength for it, like I 'ave. And if you 'ave a few beers an' maybe a fight with somebody, well, next day you sleep it off, an' nobody's any the worse. An' if you get a loggerheads with the foreman, well, you move to another site. A rovin' life, young Tony. As good as the Army, with no flippin' sergeant-majors. I can't stand bosses for long, an' that's a fact.'

Rod was silent for a moment. Then something occurred to him.

'Are they after me?' he demanded. 'The police?'

'Not that I know of,' said Tony.

'It's just as well. That Sergeant 'Awkins annoys me. I won't answer for what'll 'appen next time 'e gets across me. Nobody pushes Rod Ridgeway around an' gets away with it.'

He stood up, suddenly fierce. Gordon stepped back in alarm, and Rod's eye fell on him.

'An' you needn't think I've forgot about *you*,' he said. 'Interferin' little beggar. I can't even 'elp a pal in trouble without somebody shovin' their oar in. It's a good job for you I'm not in one of my moods this mornin', or you'd be sorry.'

'Helping a pal?' said Tony. 'You mean the business about Mr. Kite's money was Walter's affair?'

''Course it was. I'm not interested in the poor old so-and-so's savings. I can earn money if I want it, real money. Look at that, young Tony.' He rolled up his sleeve. 'Look at them muscles. Go on, feel 'em. That's my earnin'-power, that is. Strength. Now Walt Thompson, a skinny little feller like 'im, 'e relies on cunning. Artful as a cartload o' monkeys. Well, 'e was tickled to bits with this idea of 'is, gettin' the old chap to take 'is money out o' the bank an' then whippin' it off 'im quick. So I told Walt I'd 'elp 'im, seein' we was pals. A moral duty, like. But it all went wrong.'

'Where's Walter now, Rod?' Tony asked.

'Back with 'is brother Cliff, an' Cliff's wife. Walt's applied for a job on the buses. 'E's lookin' as if butter wouldn't melt in 'is mouth today. Cliff's been readin' 'im the Riot Act, tellin' 'im to be a good boy from now on. Him an' Betty, they never lose 'ope for Walt. They think 'e'll turn respectable one o' these days, an' be a credit to them. But they don't know 'im like I do. If ever there was a feller born to be in and out of trouble all 'is life, an' to get other folks involved in it too, it's Walter Thompson. . . . What time is it, Tony?'

'Not quite ten o'clock.'

'Blimey, it's a flippin' age till the pubs open. I could do with a pint now. Me throat's dry. Not used to talkin' so much. I might go round to Jones's off-licence. Back door, of course, seein' it's out of hours. They won't refuse Rod Ridgeway. . . . What are you doin' 'ere, anyway?'

'I came for Sheila's things,' said Tony. 'I was told the welfare worker had put them out, ready for me. '

'Well, 'elp yourself. I'm off.'

Rod shoved a massive fist within an inch of Gordon's face, by way of a joke, and laughed heartily to see him recoil. Next minute he was gone. They heard him clumping down the stairs.

Tony soon found Sheila's things, wrapped in a neat bundle.

'Not much to show for nine years of life,' he said. 'A few clothes, only fit for the rag-man. A stuffed cloth animal, so out-of-shape that I don't even know what it is . . .'

'It's a cat,' said Gordon. He remembered something. 'That must be Shippy. She told us her dad was a seacaptain and gave her a white Persian ship's cat to remember him by.'

'Poor old Shippy,' said Tony. 'And a battered copy of *Treasure Island*. What do you make of that, Gordon?'

'It's not what I make of it,' said Gordon. 'It's what *she* made of it.'

'Her refuge from the Jungle,' said Tony thoughtfully.

'Tony, do you think she'll always tell these tales of hers?'

'Well, I suppose as she settles down she'll not need to pretend so much. And she'll grow out of it. But I hope her imagination won't dry up altogether.'

'She said the King gave you a prize for playing the organ.'

'And how do you know he didn't?' asked Tony seriously. He held his face straight for a moment, but couldn't keep it up. 'All right,' he said. 'I admit it. I never met the King in my life.'

CHAPTER 21

The Claypits branch of the Country Library had been built in the last century as a mechanics' institute and taken over by the corporation. Gordon wasn't much impressed by it when he got out of the Alvis with Tony and Sheila. It wasn't his idea of an exciting place to visit. On his own, he wouldn't have dreamed of setting a foot inside. But this trip was at Tony's invitation. Politeness held him back from pulling a face.

They went through swing-doors, then through a room where old men snuffled and read the daily papers, then up a stairway and along a corridor painted in chocolate brown and dirty cream. At its end was a darkish room with a very small coal fire. Its walls were hung with maps and engravings, and it had racks containing old newspaper files and shelves laden with stout elderly volumes.

'This,' said Tony, 'is Local History.'

'Oh,' said Gordon. He wondered how long it was to dinner-time. But Sheila darted about delightedly among the maps. 'If I had a house with wallpaper,' she said, 'I'd strip it all off and have maps on every inch of the walls instead.'

Local History was in the care of Miss Herrick. She was a

dark-haired, smiling girl in a red jumper. She wasn't very old, and looked as if she could have been Tony's sister. She said 'Good morning' formally to Gordon, and ruffled Sheila's hair.

'Hullo, map girl,' she said. 'Did you make anything of the little sketch-map I gave you a few weeks ago?'

Gordon stared at Sheila. She blushed.

'Why, you said . . .' he began. He was on the point of reminding her that she'd told him she got her map of the River Midwell from a black-bearded stranger with a wooden leg. But an unexpected delicacy of feeling prevented him. He found he didn't want to show up any of Sheila's little pretences. Instead he stepped in as if he'd known where it came from all along.

'We found the River Midwell,' he said. 'It goes through a tunnel into the canal.'

'I thought it did. I found it afterwards on the big-scale modern map.'

'We wondered if we could see a really old map of the district,' said Tony. 'One that goes back to before it was built up. With the Vicarage on. I don't think it was the Vicarage then. But we know it was built in 1795 because it says so over the door.'

'We'll try Todd and Tempest, 1802,' said Miss Herrick at once. She went to a big cabinet that looked rather like an outsize chest of drawers, and from half-way down it she pulled out a large, ornate map. It was decorated all round the edges with pictures of old Cobchester buildings, and ladies and gentlemen in old-fashioned clothes, and horse-drawn carriages.

'There you are,' she said. And she read aloud the opening words from a panel in its top left-hand corner:

'*A True and Correct Map of the City of Cobchester, drawn by J. Todd and W. Tempest, A.D. 1802, to a Scale of Fifteen Inches to the Mile. Sold only by J. Lackenby, in St. Peter's Churchyyard, Cobchester, who also sells Snuff Boxes, Silver and Gold Plate, and all kinds of Jewellery, as Cheap as in London. N.B.—He buys Old Gold and Silver.*'

'It looks very new,' said Gordon suspiciously.

'It's a photographic copy. The original's too delicate to be in use every day.'

The children leaned over the map. Gordon was interested in spite of himself.

'Cobchester was only little then, wasn't it?' he said. 'I can see the Wigan Road. There it is. But I can't find anything else I know.'

'It's all different now,' said Miss Herrick. 'Look, it shows fields all round here, instead of streets. They're marked with the names of the owners.'

'And here's the Vicarage!' said Sheila, triumphant. She pointed a small finger. Gordon noticed how clean that finger was. It didn't seem natural in Sheila. But it must be part of the new way of life.

'How do you know it's the Vicarage?' he asked. 'It doesn't say so. It says ... it says ...' He peered at the small old-fashioned writing. 'Hill fide. What does "Hill fide" mean?'

'That's "Hill Side", spelt with the long S they used in those days,' said Miss Herrick. 'It's the only house for half a mile around, and yes, it must be the one that's now the Vicarage.'

'You were quick to spot that,' said Tony to Sheila.

'She's seen it before, haven't you, pet?' said Miss Herrick. Sheila blushed again.

Gordon refrained once more from saying anything, though he began to feel there was a good deal that Sheila hadn't told him.

'There's something in brackets after the words "Hill Side",' he said. 'It's very tiny. I can't read it.'

'I'll bring a magnifying-glass,' said Miss Herrick, and did. Tony spelt the letters out with difficulty.

'Charles Culver, Esquire,' he said. And he read out the whole description. 'Hill Side. Charles Culver Esquire. Well, there you are, you two. There's your "C.C."'

This time Gordon wasn't able to keep tactfully quiet.

'You said Captain Cutlass,' he reminded Sheila.

'Well, it's nearly that,' said Sheila. 'Charles Culver and Captain Cutlass, it's almost the same. The map people might have made a mistake.'

'I don't think so, Sheila,' said Tony firmly.

Sheila was poring over the map again.

'Look, the river's there,' she said. 'I told you it was. Before they put it underground. And all those fields between the Vicarage and the river are marked with the owner's name, too. And it's Captain Cutlass again.'

'Charles Culver,' Gordon corrected her.

'So he must have owned all this land round here. And look, there *is* a tiny island in the river. Lower down. Just about where the canal would be now. Isn't it, Miss Herrick?'

'You're too quick for me, Sheila.... Yes, I suppose it would be somewhere around where the Canal Company premises are.'

'I knew it was. I bet it's our island.'

'I bet it's not,' said Gordon with conviction. 'Our island was something the Canal Company built.'

'Well, who's been right about everything else?' asked Sheila. 'Me. I have, haven't I, Miss Herrick? Haven't I, Tony? I have. And there's an island there on the map. And it says—what does it say, Gordon?'

Gordon had borrowed the magnifying-glass from Miss Herrick.

'It says "Captain Culver's if land",' he said.

'Island!' said Sheila. 'That proves it. He was a captain and there was an island and it's our Pirate's Island!'

Gordon opened his mouth to speak. There were some very doubtful links in this chain, he felt. Especially, he was quite sure that the island in the canal—that sour patch of soil surrounded by indigo brickwork, where once the supports of a footbridge had been—was of the Canal Company's making, and not something left over from the days when the Midwell was a proper river. But he caught Tony's eye and decided yet again to keep tactfully quiet.

'All right,' he said. 'All right. It's our island.' And then a further point struck him.

'Who says Captain Culver was a pirate?' he asked.

'It's in a book,' said Sheila. 'Isn't it, Miss Herrick? A book about all kinds of people who used to live in Cobchester.'

'I believe we found something about him in Bowden's *Local Worthies*,' said Miss Herrick. 'Just a minute, let's look him up.' She brought three solid, red-backed books out of the shelves. 'Here's old Bowden. Quite a local worthy himself. He was writing in about the 1860's. The index is at the back. Cubbins, Cuddlesham, Cuggett. . . . Marvellous names some of these people had. Oh, here we are. Culver, Charles. Volume Two, page 334.' She turned over some pages. 'Shall I read it out? All right. This is what it says:

'*About this time there came to the city Mr. Charles Culver, who had spent most of his life at sea and was widely reputed to have been a pirate . . .*'

'There you are!' said Sheila.

'*. . . though this he sternly denied.*'

'There *you* are!' said Gordon.

'... *It was however established that he had been master of several merchantmen in his time, and had held letters of marque during the early part of the Napoleonic wars.*'

'What were letters of marque?' asked Gordon.

'They were a kind of wartime licence given to masters of merchant ships to plunder enemy vessels.'

'So he *was* a pirate!' said Sheila.

'Well, a sort-of-a-pirate, yes. A privateer is the proper word.'

'And he might have had a treasure!'

'He might,' said Miss Herrick.

'And he might have buried it on Pirate's Island.'

'I suppose so,' said Tony. 'But, you know, Sheila, if he'd had a treasure, and if he got it safely home to England, why would he need to bury it?'

'They *always* buried their treasure,' Sheila said. But then, grasping Tony's point, she fell silent.

'I expect, if he did have any treasure, he'd sell it,' Tony said. Sheila revived at once.

'Oh, yes, he'd sell it to Mr. Lackenby who had maps and snuff-boxes and all those other lovely things. It said he bought old gold and silver. I expect he bought pirates' treasures, too.'

'Perhaps,' said Tony, smiling. 'Perhaps Captain Culver sold his treasure and bought the house. So really the house would be his treasure then.'

'And he'd keep the chest as a souvenir,' said Sheila, satisfied.

Gordon yawned. He was feeling distinctly hungry by now.

'I've been reading on a bit,' said Miss Herrick. 'It seems Captain Culver built himself this house, Hill Side, and lived there for years with his daughter Emily, who was supposed to be beautiful and poetic and suffering from an unhappy love affair. And then he died, and Emily's admirer came back from sea and married her, and the house passed to Captain Culver's nephew George. Bowden calls him "a convivial gentleman". I expect that means he drank. And he sold all the land for housing at the start of the nineteenth-century boom. And that's all that Bowden had to say about the Culvers.'

'And I can finish it off,' said Tony, 'because about 1870 the Church people found themselves with a huge overpopulated area in need of spiritual care, so they built St. Jude's and they bought the house for a Vicarage. Which is what it still is.'

'It that all?' asked Gordon. 'My mum doesn't like me to be late for meals.'

114

'You have no soul, Gordon,' said Tony, smiling. 'Only a stomach.'

'Don't be horrid to him, Tony,' said Sheila. 'Gordon's a doer of things, aren't you, Gordon? He's ever such a good doer of things. He isn't really a hearer about things or a reader about things.'

'It was very interesting,' said Gordon politely.

'It was fascinating to me,' said Tony. 'And you see how the facts can be just as much fun as wild imaginings.'

'Yes,' said Sheila. 'At least, *nearly* as much fun.'

Gordon thought of the roast beef and Yorkshire pudding his mother had promised for his dinner.

'I hope there's baked potatoes with it,' he said.

CHAPTER 22

'My goodness, what a diference from when we first saw her,' said Mrs. Dobbs. 'She looks—she looks—well, I don't know what to say. She looks *nice*.'

'Kids are much the same underneath,' said Mr. Dobbs, 'whether you wash their faces and put a clean apron on 'em, or whether you just let 'em run around dirty. I don't notice any change in Sheila myself. Maybe the Vicarage suits her better than the Shambles, seeing she's a bit out of this world. But it doesn't make any odds to me. Now if you said *Gordon* had changed, I'd agree with you. That lad's beginning to shape. And not before time, either.'

Mrs. Dobbs pursed her lips. She didn't approve of some of Gordon's new ways. But in a moment her face softened again. She and Mrs. Dobbs were standing in the shop doorway, watching as Gordon and Sheila disappeared down Hibiscus Street. 'Don't they look sweet, going off for a quiet walk together?'

'Now listen here, Elsie,' said Mr. Dobbs. 'I'm glad to have that kiddie around, as you well know. But I'll tell you one thing. Lads of twelve don't play out with little lasses of nine for long. Gordon'll be wanting to get together with lads of his own age. And he won't want her tagging on. I'm just warning you, that's the way things are. You can't run children's lives to suit your own fancy.'

'You don't know Gordon at all,' said Mrs. Dobbs.

'I know him better than you think,' said her husband.

Gordon and Sheila were on their way to the canal-bank. They walked along the tow-path, under the viaduct, up the alleyway that ran between the railway and the canal premises, and into Wharf Street. They came to the painter's yard where, weeks ago, they'd climbed the wall for their first sight of the River Midwell pouring from its tunnel into the canal, and their first sight of Pirate's Island. At the entrance to the yard, the chalked notice still said: *Keep out. This means you.* But there was nobody around.

And the ladder was still lying in a corner.

'Come on,' said Sheila. 'Be quick!'

'What about that chap who ordered us off?' said Gordon uneasily. 'What if he comes?'

'Oh, he won't. We shan't be a minute. You're not frightened, Gordon, are you? Let's get the ladder up.'

They leaned the ladder against the wall, climbed up, and looked over once more at the canal, the deserted wharves, the River Midwell splashing from its tunnel, and the island.

'Seems just the same to me,' said Gordon. 'Nobody's even filled in the hole on Pirate's Island. There's still that heap of soil we dug out. And look, there's our raft down there, just where we left it. Do you want another trip?'

Sheila shuddered.

'No,' she said. 'I don't want to go on the canal any more, ever in my life. I just wanted to have a last look at the island. It's sort of empty, isn't it? As if the treasure had gone.'

'Which it has,' said Gordon. 'You can't have forgotten yet. We dug it up. Mr. Kite's money.'

'Yes. I suppose it's the end of that story. I suppose it wasn't true about a real pirate's treasure. At least, not quite true. Nearly true.'

'Still,' said Gordon, 'a lot happened that wouldn't have happened but for us. I like making things happen.'

Then he remembered the man who'd caught them here before, and the threats he'd made.

'Let's get down from here,' he said, 'and be away before anyone comes.'

They climbed down the ladder and put it back in its corner. Gordon didn't breath freely till they were back through the alleyway and on the tow-path, heading for home.

'What's it like at the Vicarage?' he asked them.

Sheila looked doubtful.

'Mrs. Wallace is ever so particular,' she said. 'I have to wash my hands before meals. And I go to bed at eight.'

'But are you happy there?'

'I don't know. It feels a bit odd. I expect I'll be happy when I get used to it. It's funny having to go in for meals at set times. But at least I know there'll *be* a meal. And the house is full of books, hundreds of books.'

Gordon didn't think this was a huge attraction.

'But what about Mrs. Wallace?' he asked. 'She's so tall and sort of sharp. I'd be scared of her.'

'But she's kind, Gordon. She can't help being sharp. Don't you think it's kind to take *me*, when her own children are grown up?' 'I expect she likes you,' said Gordon.

'Yes, I expect she does,' said Sheila with satisfaction.

'But why did she sell the chest?' This was the last of the mysteries that had puzzled Gordon, and he hadn't liked to ask about it.

'Well, I'd have thought you'd have guessed,' said Sheila. 'She sold it to help me and the other children. The Wallaces aren't well off, you know. It costs ever so much to keep that Vicarage going. But she used to send things for us to eat, nearly every day. And then a few weeks ago the rent wasn't paid and we were going to be turned out. There was three pounds owing. And Mrs. Wallace hadn't got it at first, but later she gave it me. And it must have come from selling the chest.'

Gordon was surprised. He'd thought of Mr. and Mrs. Wallace as being rich.

'So you see,' said Sheila. 'You can't tell how nice people really are by just looking at them. Especially Mrs. Wallace.'

'You can tell Tony Boyd's nice by just looking at him,' said Gordon.

'Oh, yes!' said Sheila with enthusiasm. 'And Tony comes ever so often. That's one of the best things of all.'

She leaned towards Gordon confidentially.

'Shall I tell you something?' she said. 'I'm going to marry

Tony when I grow up.'

'What, you?' said Gordon. He laughed. 'Tony's ever so old.'

'He's seventeen.'

'And you're nine. He's nearly twice your age.'

'I'll be ten soon. And he'll still be seventeen. And when I'm twenty he'll be twenty-seven. That's not much difference.'

'It's a long time for him to wait,' said Gordon.

'People do wait long times,' said Sheila. 'Just think of Captain Cutlass's daughter.'

'Mr. Culver's daughter, you mean.'

'All right. His daughter Emily. All those years, going for long walks across country with her father and her . . . and her faithful dog, she had a faithful dog, I'm sure she would . . . and she waited and waited while her own true love was at sea . . .' The distant look was in Sheila's eyes. 'And at last he came home. "Emily," he said, "for all these many years I have thought of nothing but you. And now that I have made my fortune I want you to be my bride . . ." '

'You're as barmy as ever,' said Gordon tolerantly. And then, 'Look, there's Tim Ridgeway, and Alan Manning, and that lot.'

'Well, you're still not afraid,' said Sheila.

Gordon thought perhaps he wasn't afraid now, though he was a bit uncertain about it. There were half a dozen lads and there was only one of him. He'd rather not have met them just now.

'Why, it's Porky Dobbs!' said Alan Manning, the leader of the gang. 'How do, Porky? What price sausages today?'

'Here, Tim, here's your pal!' said Doug Staples.

Tim turned red and looked the other way.

'Don't be scared of him, Tim!' said Alan, grinning.

'I'm not scared of him,' said Tim. But he sounded subdued. It struck Gordon that Tim had been going through a rough patch. It wasn't so much that he, Gordon, had beaten Tim and banged his head in the gutter. That was a small matter. But Tim had lost the glory and protection of an older brother, for Rod had now gone off to some huge building-site in Yorkshire. And Tim had come back from his uncle's to his own home— but it wasn't much of a home. Gordon could almost feel sorry for Tim.

Doug Staples wasn't sensitive to thoughts like these.

'Go on, Tim!' he urged. 'Show him you're not scared. Bash

him!'

Tim and Gordon looked at each other. Neither of them seemed anxious to fight. Doug began to get impatient.

'Get on with it, Tim!' he demanded. 'Teach him a lesson!'

'Why don't you teach him a lesson yourself, Doug?' asked Alan Manning.

But although Doug had been eager to start others fighting, it didn't look as if he was keen to put his own fists up. He stepped back a pace.

'Or else leave him alone,' said Alan. He turned to Gordon. 'Here, Porky, you can come with us if you like. We're going down to the wharves. We found a way into one of them empty warehouses.'

The wharves seemed like home ground to Gordon now. In spite of his experiences, he found he was quite willing to go down there and explore with the lads. He could show them the raft, and the tunnel, and the island. He could tell the tale. He could impress them. He could be one of them if he wanted.

'But what about *her*?' he said, indicating Sheila.

'Oh, we're not having any little lasses.'

Gordon hesitated.

'It's all right,' said Sheila. 'I'll have to go now, anyway. Mrs. Wallace told me not to be long.'

'I'll just take her home,' Gordon told them. 'I won't be five minutes. Then I'll come back.'

'Oh, you needn't bother,' said Sheila. Her nose was in the air, her tone of voice was hoity-toity. For nine years old, she seemed absurdly grown-up. 'I know my way home all right. Never mind, Gordon. I don't need you. Off you go and play with the lads.'

TITLES IN THIS SERIES

DEVIL'S HILL NAN CHAUNCY
THE EAGLE OF THE NINTH ROSEMARY SUTCLIFF
EARTHQUAKE ANDREW SALKEY
THE EDGE OF THE CLOUD K. M. PEYTON
FLAMBARDS K. M. PEYTON
FLAMBARDS IN SUMMER K. M. PEYTON
FLY-BY-NIGHT K. M. PEYTON
A GRASS ROPE WILLIAM MAYNE
HURRICANE ANDREW SALKEY
IN SPITE OF ALL TERROR HESTER BURTON
THE INTRUDER JOHN ROWE TOWNSEND
JUMPER NICHOLAS KALASHNIKOFF
KNIGHT CRUSADER RONALD WELCH
THE LITTLE BOOKROOM ELEANOR FARJEON
LITTLE KATIA E. M. ALMEDINGEN
MINNOW ON THE SAY A. PHILIPPA PEARCE
NORDY BANK SHEENA PORTER
PASTURES OF THE BLUE CRANE H. F. BRINSMEAD
PIPPI GOES ABOARD ASTRID LINDGREN
PIPPI IN THE SOUTH SEAS ASTRID LINDGREN
PIPPI LONGSTOCKING ASTRID LINDGREN
PIRATE'S ISLAND JOHN ROWE TOWNSEND
RIDE A NORTHBOUND HORSE RICHARD WORMSER
A SAPPHIRE FOR SEPTEMBER H. F. BRINSMEAD
SIRGA RENÉ GUILLOT
TANGARA NAN CHAUNCY
TIGER IN THE BUSH NAN CHAUNCY
TOM'S MIDNIGHT GARDEN A. PHILIPPA PEARCE
WARRIOR SCARLET ROSEMARY SUTCLIFF
WHEN JAYS FLY TO BARBMO MARGARET BALDERSON